"The in...
the murder is now
officially closed."

I couldn't believe my ears. "And he's actually confessed, has he, Inspector?"

Inspector MacDonald looked decidedly uncomfortable. "There was no confession, Mrs. Hudson," he informed me. "The gentleman in question is dead. Hanged himself, ma'am. The man made no oral confession to anyone, nor was there a note of any kind left."

"Then what you're saying," I said, "is that you or, for that matter, Scotland Yard, have no idea how the murder was actually carried out."

It seemed to me that an unsolved crime was now to be swept under the judicial rug.

Most Baffling, Mrs. Hudson

SYDNEY HOSIER

AVON BOOKS ◆ NEW YORK

AVON BOOKS
A division of
The Hearst Corporation
1350 Avenue of the Americas
New York, New York 10019

Copyright © 1998 by J. S. Hosier
Published by arrangement with the author
Visit our website at http://www.AvonBooks.com
Library of Congress Catalog Card Number: 97-93791
ISBN: 0-380-79216-8

First Avon Books Printing: January 1998

AVON TRADEMARK REG. U.S. PAT. OFF. AND IN OTHER COUNTRIES, MARCA REGISTRADA, HECHO EN U.S.A.

Printed in the U.S.A.

WCD   10   9   8   7   6   5   4   3   2   1

Contents

ONE

Invitation to a Murder

~ "TOAD-IN-THE-HOLE THEN, IS it, Mrs. Hudson?"

"If you've no objection, Mrs. Warner," I answered curtly, setting the sausages off to one side before removing a large wooden mixing bowl from the cupboard and placing it on the counter before me.

As my companion and I had not been on the best of terms of late, taking it upon herself to act as overseer as I set about to prepare this most singular of English dishes, was hardly conducive to alleviating the existing tension between us. Nevertheless, I carried on by humming away a merry little tune to myself as if to show I was completely oblivious to her presence. After pouring in the required amount of flour, all the while, I might add, under her watchful

1

eye, I deftly cracked an egg and added its contents to the bowl.

"Using just the one egg then, are you, Mrs. Hudson?"

It should be noted that since our tiff we had taken to addressing each other by surname only. "Of *course*, one egg," I stated forcefully. "I always—"

"Aye, well, you do as you like," she interjected in a most condescending manner. " 'Course, with me, now, I always add two, the proper way, like. Gives the batter more body, you might say. Then, when it's added to the sausages—"

It was now my turn to interrupt. "The *proper* way? Mrs. Warner," I announced through gritted teeth while trying to maintain a measure of self-control, "I have been making toad-in-the-hole for more years than I jolly well care to remember and in all that time I have yet to receive one single word of complaint. Now, if you don't mind—"

"Oh, well," she declared, "it's easy enough to see you're all sixes and nines, ain't it? And don't think I don't know the reason why, Emma Hudson. It's 'bout that ad in the *Times*, like as not."

She was right, of course. The ad to which she had referred was the one she had taken upon herself to place in the London *Times* advertising our services as consulting detectives. As I had told her, as consulting detectives, she would have been well advised to consult with me first as to the merit of it.

Although I knew she had nothing but the best of intentions, I was nevertheless under the impression, as I believed she was as well, that we would take on only those cases that came our way by happenstance and then only if they were of interest to us. It was never my intention to make a career out of it. Nor could I if I had wanted to do so. My household chores plus seeing to the needs of my two upstairs lodgers, Mr. Holmes and Doctor Watson, were quite enough, thank you very much, for a woman of my age. Though I am not in any way denigrating my live-in companion's own contribution to the upkeep of 221B Baker Street.

In any event, as I say, the upshot of it all being that a strained relationship existed between the two of us for the better part of three days. Such was my vanity I believed her ad would produce a plethora of replies.

"And how do you propose we handle all those who will write in to ask for assistance?" I asked, while setting about the pouring of milk and the adding of salt into the bowl before me. "Are you prepared to send letters of explanation," I continued on, now lightly stirring the contents, "as to why we cannot address ourselves to their particular problem? There are only so many hours in a day, Violet Warner, as well you know."

The reader will note that as our icy reserve began to thaw, we each took to addressing the other by both Christian and surname.

"Aye, well, be that as it may, the thing of it was it's been that quiet round here of late. And what harm would it do to stir things up a bit, eh? That's what I thought. Can't see us gettin' weighed down by replies from it though, as some I could mention."

"Well, we'll soon see, won't we?" I replied on hearing the front doorbell. "That'll be the post, like as not," I added, while in the process of wiping fingers of flour clean on my apron.

" 'Ere, now, never you mind, I'll see to it," she volunteered. "More than likely the poor man's weighed down with a sackful of letters," was her parting shot as she made her way down the hallway. "And all for us, no doubt."

Taking advantage of her absence, I placed the previously lightly cooked sausages into a pan, poured the batter in and around them, and quickly popped it into the oven.

Back she came, waltzing into the kitchen with a smug little smile on her face and waving two envelopes about, which she placed with a theatrical flourish on the table before airily announcing, "That's the lot of 'em."

Feeling somewhat chagrined on seeing what I had believed would be an avalanche of mail to be no more than a trickle of two, I managed to mumble something to the effect that "no doubt there'll be more." Though if memory serves me correctly they were the only two replies we would ever receive from my companion's placement of the ad.

We took our place at the table. "You first," I said, indicating either one of the two envelopes before us. She took the one nearest to her, deftly slicing it open with the aid of my bread knife. I in turn followed suit.

"Well, we've come a-cropper on this one, and no mistake," she announced after silently reading over its contents.

"How so?"

"It's from some bloke what wants us to find his lost corgi." She made a face. "Wants us to find his ruddy dog, does he—can you imagine? It'll be cats up a tree, next."

"I think we can safely set that one aside," I said.

" 'Ere, Em, I know," she announced with a sly little wink, "why not reseal this here letter and shove it under Mr. Sherlock Holmes's door, eh? Oh, what wouldn't I give to see his face when he reads it."

"Oh, Vi," I laughed, "you are a caution."

The reader will note that we were once more back on a first-name basis. Our tiff at best being all but forgotten. What silly creatures we humans are.

"I hope yours is more to our liking," spoke Vi as I spread the one remaining letter out before me.

"At least it's quality paper," I mused, noting its texture with a gentle rub twixt forefinger and thumb.

"I daresay our Mr. Holmes could tell us not only where it was made but who made it, like as not," stated Vi in a confessed admiration for the man upstairs.

"No doubt," I smiled. "However, our primary interest lies in its message rather than its origin of manufacture."

"Aye, right enough."

"A woman's hand," I noted aloud on scanning its contents. "The penmanship is excellent."

"But what's it say, eh?" was my companion's exasperated response. "That's what I'd like to know 'fore I gets any older."

I suppose I must have looked somewhat incredulous as I read, for, as I set the letter down, Vi asked whatever was the matter. "You're not going to believe this," I said, for I could scarcely believe it myself, "but the letter is from Mrs. Bramwell. Mrs. Jane Bramwell."

For a moment or two Vi's face remained a questioning blank. Then: " 'Ere, not the same Mrs. Bramwell whose husband—?"

"The very same."

"Coo!"

Coo, indeed. To have the woman, whose husband's murder was still front page news a week after the crime, request a meeting in regard to our services, left me momentarily stunned. Violet snatched the letter up and with eyes darting from word to word read aloud in part the woman's concluding lines . . . " 'with respect to the terrible tragedy that has befallen my husband of which I'm sure the newspapers have kept you and all of England fully aware.' "

"Fully aware, she says!" exclaimed Violet. "I should say so! Who hasn't read about the Invisible Man what shot that poor Mr. Bramwell, eh? And him, like me, being from Manchester, and all."

"Not a kin of yours, was he?" I asked facetiously, knowing from the newspaper accounts that the man had been a wealthy industrialist.

"Not ruddy likely. It's just that there's not a soul in Manchester what hasn't heard of the Bramwell Textile and Manufacturing Company. Seems like everybody I knew worked there at one time or another. 'Course I was just a tyke at the time old Mr. Bramwell ran it. And then to read only last week 'bout young Mr. Bramwell who'd taken over the business when the old gentleman passed on, being murdered and all . . ." Her voice drifted off into a despairing sigh.

"You realize of course," I announced, interrupting her reverie, "that the story of an invisible man being responsible for the death of Edgar Bramwell is simply a way for some of our more, shall I say, imaginative newspapers to increase their circulation.''

"Well, yes, 'course I do," she huffed. "Still, it does make a body wonder. I mean, what with nobody seein' who shot him and them all standing there in the same room at the time it happened, like. Well, I ask you—''

"Please, don't ask," I answered with a half-hearted chuckle, "for I haven't the foggiest. They say the Bramwell murder is one of the most baffling ever encountered within the annals of English crime. Of course, there again, that's the newspapers for you. Still, all in all, if the facts as related are true, one would be hard pressed to disagree.''

"Maybe," ventured Vi, "there's summat the police are holding back. Know more than they're lettin' on, like. They do that sometimes," she added very knowingly.

"One can only hope," I answered. "Otherwise we're back to the theory of an invisible man. We may," I added after a momentary pause, "be in over our heads on this one if we agree to enter into it.''

"It wouldn't be the first time," was my companion's quick retort. "But," she added, "what I don't understand is why this here Mrs. Bramwell never got in touch with the likes of Mr. Holmes and Doctor Watson. Give their eye-teeth, they would, to be involved in summat like this.''

"That," I stated, "is just one of the questions I intend to ask.''

"We're taking it on then, are we?''

"Well, let's hear what she has to say, at least. As it stands now," I smiled, "it's either the Bramwell murder or the case of the missing corgi.''

"Aye," chuckled Vi in response, "and you know how much that'd pay. See the address on Mrs. Bramwell's letter, did you? Mayfair, no less. All very posh, I must say."

"Well, you'd hardly expect the Bramwell residence to be located in Whitechapel, now would you?"

"When was it she said she wanted to see us?" she asked, ignoring my comment and seeking the answer for herself by returning her attention back to the letter.

"On the eighteenth," I spoke up. "At two o'clock." I turned my head and squinted at the calendar on the far wall of the kitchen. "That would make it . . ."

"Today!" exclaimed Violet. "It's the eighteenth, today."

"Good lord," I moaned, "you're right. We've scarcely time to make ourselves presentable if we're to be there by two this afternoon."

My old friend's face sagged in disappointment. "I can't make it," was her sullen announcement.

"What? Why ever not?"

"I've an appointment myself, I have," she moaned. "At the dentist. If I don't show up he charges me all the same. Ruddy begger, that he is."

"It's still bothering you then, is it?" I asked, knowing she had been in intermittent pain for the better part of two weeks.

"Aye, acts up, it does, now and then," she answered. At which point she inserted a finger in her mouth and began poking it around. "It's way in back," she announced in a gurgle of words. "It's probably upset 'cause it misses its mates on either side.''

It was a quip that belied her dread of dentists. "Perhaps," I said, in the hope of belaying her fears, "you'll be lucky this time in not needing it pulled. In any event, m'girl," I added in finality, "it seems I shall have to keep our appointment with Mrs. Bramwell myself.''

We made ourselves presentable for each of our respective outings and had a quick lunch consisting of no more than a tea and an egg salad sandwich. I set about removing our supper for the night from the oven. And very nice it looked too, I must say. Two eggs, indeed! Done now to a golden brown, when reheated it would, I'm sure, garner warm praise from even Mr. Holmes; a most persnickety eater, at best.

It was by then thirty minutes past one and, with the parlor clock chiming out the half hour, I said my goodbyes to Violet and watched as she took off, none too cheerfully, for the dentist. As for myself, I gave one last primp to my hair in the hall mirror, placed my wide-brimmed hat with its sprig of artificial flowers on my head, donned my coat, and off I went as well.

On my arrival I alighted from the cab and, feeling slightly intimidated by the fashionable row of houses that fronted the street, foolishly added a much too generous tip to my fare. After pausing momentarily to recheck the house number with the one I had written down, I mounted the three steps leading up to the black lacquered door and knocked.

As I waited, I noticed that various people passing by were slowing down in their walk to gaze up and gawk at me. Did I look so out of place? It was then the thought struck me as to what the whispered conversations might be. "That's it," I imagined them saying, "that's the house where the murder took place." "Wonder who *she* is?" "Bramwell's mother, like as not." "They say he was shot by an invisible man." "Oh, yes, and I'm the king of the fairies, I am. What rot." While lost in these imaginings, a policeman appeared on the scene, his presence being all that was needed to send the gaggle of onlookers on their way.

"Have business inside, do you, madam?" he asked, turning his attention to me as I continued my stance on the top step.

Before my answer could be given the door was swung open by a rather pleasant-faced young man who, by his attire, I rightly judged to be the butler. "Mrs. Warner, is it?" he asked. "Please, come in."

"Hudson," I corrected him. "Mrs. Hudson."

"It's all right, Officer," he called out to the constable before quickly closing the door behind us, "the lady is expected."

Once inside, he offered up his apologies for the hasty entrance by admitting the house had become the object of the curious of late. I understood perfectly and told him as much.

"Am I not right in thinking," he asked, on taking my coat and hat, "that Mrs. Bramwell was expecting a Mrs. Warner, as well?"

After my informing him that she had a prior engagement, he left to inform his mistress of my arrival, returning shortly thereafter to escort me into her presence within the study.

I walked into a room illuminated by gaslight. The

afternoon sun was blocked by drapes pulled shut across a window that served as a backdrop to the large ornate desk in front of it.

Behind the desk sat Mrs. Jane Bramwell.

She rose and extended her hand in greeting as did I. After an exchange of pleasantries and the offering of my condolences I was offered a seat in the green leather chair that sat at a slightly right angle to the front of the desk.

"I understand from Martin that Mrs. Warner won't be able to join us. Work as a pair, do you?" she asked pleasantly enough.

I answered in the affirmative, adding on Vi's behalf that her absence was due to a prior medical appointment which, I thought, sounded a trifle more professional than simply stating she had to pay a visit to the dentist. I received a sympathetic nod of understanding.

"Yes, well, I suppose we should begin then, shouldn't we?" she stated rhetorically while nervously twisting at the chain of a lovely cameo pendant that hung down over the bodice of her dress. She was clearly ill at ease, though I suppose that was understandable after what she had been through. "I thought it best if we spoke in here," she began. "In my husband's—" She paused long enough to correct herself. "In my late husband's study. More businesslike, you see. And I must be more businesslike, mustn't I, now that—" With a heavy sigh she let the sentence hang. "Forgive the drapes being drawn," she announced quite unexpectedly, hoping, I presumed, that a change in subject matter would help her emotionally to carry on. "But the thing of it is, we've had so much trouble, you see, with people peering in through the window. Though what on earth they expect to see—'' This time, her voice trembled and she bit at her lower lip. ''I'm sorry,'' she said at last, ''I'm afraid I'm making rather a mess of all this, aren't I?''

I put forward the suggestion that perhaps it might be best if I came at another time.

''No, no,'' she implored. ''Please, just give me a minute or two to compose myself.''

I took that minute to study the woman opposite me.

A pretty enough young thing she was. No more than thirty, if that, with light auburn hair so perfectly set that one would be hard put to ever imagine it in disarray. The complexion of the oval face, complete with a fine little tilt to the nose, was clear but pale. The eyes of sea-green, rimmed by the most extraordinary long lashes, should have been her best feature but were marred by the melancholy sadness I saw within them. Strange, I thought, for one so young. Oh, it would be easy enough to ascribe it to the events of the past few days, yet I couldn't help but feel it went deeper than that. My thoughts were interrupted by her asking if we might begin again.

''Perhaps,'' I said, ''we could start off by you telling me why you feel the need for private detectives to enter into this most unhappy event. I would imagine that Scotland Yard with all its resources and manpower—''

''Scotland Yard,'' interjected the lady, ''and I speak in particular of a certain Inspector MacDonald, believes me to be the guilty party.''

''Surely not!'' I exclaimed. ''Have you been formally charged?''

"Nothing so official as that," she was quick to state. "But I know he does, Mrs. Hudson. Three times since the shooting took place he's been here questioning me. Never coming right out with it, mind you, but insinuating it in so many words that I—oh, Mrs. Hudson," she groaned, "it's all been so dreadful. You can't imagine."

I put it to her that the man was merely doing his job. And that job was to continue to question all those who were present within the room until an answer to this most baffling murder could be found. She shook her head in complete disagreement with me.

"Don't you see," she stated in all earnestness, "if Scotland Yard believes me guilty then what chance do I have they will, as you say, use all their resources and manpower in tracking down the real murderer?"

"And so you thought," I replied, leaning thoughtfully back in my chair, "you'd hire private detectives to get to the bottom of it."

"Exactly!" she exclaimed, reaching up and clutching the pendant so tightly the luckless thing came off in her hand. "Oh, bother," she moaned. "The clasp," she added by way of explanation, "it's defective. Now, as to the mystery of my husband's death," she added, while in the process of refastening it, "you will look into it, won't you, Mrs. Hudson?"

How could I not? Here was a murder that, on the face of it, defied all logic. As Vi had stated, my two upstairs lodgers would have given their eye-teeth to have been asked in on it. And here it was offered up on a silver platter, as it were, not to the Holmes

and Watson duo but to the team of Hudson and Warner. And although I fairly tingled at the prospect of
it, I assured her in a most calm and professional
manner that not only would I accept but that both
Mrs. Warner and myself would do our utmost in
ferreting out the one responsible for such a dastardly
deed. "But," I added, "one thing puzzles me, Mrs.
Bramwell. In your quest for a private detective, why
did you not seek contact with Mr. Sherlock Holmes?
You've no doubt heard of him. His reputation in the
solving of crimes is legendary."

"Indeed I have heard of him," she announced.
"But you see, Mrs. Hudson, Sherlock Holmes is a
man."

That set me aback. "I—don't . . . ?"

"The thing of it is," she confessed, "I'd feel
more comfortable in having someone of my own sex
look into it. Don't misjudge me," she added with a
little laugh, "I'm no man-hater. But men can be so
detached. They tend to see everything in black and
white, as it were. As I say," she reiterated, "I'd feel
more at ease having someone such as yourself on
my side. We women must stick together, don't you
see."

Such was her reasoning and, although I could
agree with her in part, I did not hesitate to inform
her that if I was to be in her employ my function
would be to assess all the facts, follow up on any
clue, establish motive, and question any and all for
the purpose of credibility and information, herself
included.

"My dear Mrs. Hudson," she assured me most
emphatically, "you'll have no trouble with me on
that score. Pray, ask anything you wish."

Delving my hand into my purse and removing both pencil and note pad, I put it to her that although many of my questions will have already undoubtedly been asked by the police, it was information I needed, nonetheless. I then began by asking her for the names of those present within the room on the night in question, excluding herself and her late husband. Her shoulders heaved in conjunction with a resigned sigh as she set about rattling off the names.

"David MacPhail, his wife, Patricia, Arthur Moore, his fiancée—"

"One moment, please, Mrs. Bramwell," I sang out good-naturedly, "not so fast. Now then, I believe the first names you mentioned were that of a David MacPhail and his wife, Patricia?"

"I'm sorry. Yes, that's right."

"Who are—?"

"How'd you mean?"

"In relation to yourself and your late husband."

"Oh, I see. Yes, well, my husband and David were old school chums who have managed to keep in touch over the years. Actually, the MacPhails arrived back in London only a fortnight ago. That was one of the reasons why Edgar threw the party. To welcome them back, don't you see."

"*One* of the reasons?"

"Edgar did love his parties so," she replied with a wistful smile.

"And the MacPhails," I asked. "They do not reside in England, then?"

"No. David's in rubber."

"Pardon?"

"In rubber," she repeated. "Owns and operates a large rubber plantation somewhere out in the Far

East from what I understand. Oh, I say, would you care for a tea? I could ring—'' She reached for a small silver bell on the desk.

"Thank you, no. Not for me," I answered. Although I would have dearly loved one, I thought it best to press on. "You mentioned also, an Arthur—?"

"Moore. Yes, Arthur Moore, who was until recently the general manager of Bramwell Textile."

"How recently?"

"I really couldn't say, exactly. No more than a month, at best."

"Retired, is he?"

"No."

"Then—?"

"I, ah—I believe the official explanation is a leave of absence."

On sensing an uneasiness on her part, I looked up from my writing and saw her fidget slightly. "Is there something you're omitting?" I asked.

"No, nothing," she answered, a little too quickly. "In any event, it would have no bearing on your investigation."

I stated simply but firmly that she let me be the judge of that, adding that this was not an over-the-garden-fence chit-chat but an inquiry into a murder.

"Very well then, Mrs. Hudson," she replied a little coolly, "I have said I would answer your questions and I shall. Mr. Moore," she began, "is not on a leave of absence from the company. My husband had no other choice than to ask for his resignation due to the man's alcohol problem. Though I can assure you, it was a decision Edgar agonized over not unduly. For not only did he have respect for the man but, Arthur Moore, in all but name, *was* Bramwell Textile. Unfortunately, and I tell you this with the wish that it go no farther than this room, the company has gone into a sharp financial decline within the last year, due in no small measure, Edgar believed, to the gentleman's excessive drinking. Not that he wasn't given repeated warnings, mind you," she added, in spirited defense of her husband.

"And yet," I queried, "how is it that, being dismissed, he is invited to a party given by your husband?"

"Out of loyalty to his years of service, I would imagine. You see, Arthur Moore worked for many years for old Mr. Bramwell, as well."

"Yes," I answered, still a little puzzled, "that would explain your husband's invitation but not Mr. Moore's acceptance of it. One would assume the man himself would not look so kindly on the one responsible for his dismissal."

A shadow of a smile played on her lips. "We Bramwells are not without influence in the business community," she said.

"And Mr. Moore is not one to burn his bridges behind him," I added as a followup to her statement. I received another slight smile in return. "Mrs. Bramwell," I thought to ask, "how is it that you and your husband took up residency here in London rather than in Manchester where the business is located?"

"I'm afraid," she confessed, "my husband was not the hands-on businessman his father was. As I say, everything was left pretty much under Mr. Moore's supervision. Though, to give Edgar credit, he did journey to the mill at least three times a year for an overall appraisal of the business and he did keep up a running correspondence with Arthur as well. That way," she added, "my husband was free to do in London what he did best."

"And that would be—?"

"To live like a gentleman."

Was there a touch of sarcasm in the voice? Not knowing quite how to respond or if indeed whether a response from me was required, I pressed on. "You mentioned that Mr. Moore's intended bride was also present. She is—?"

"Prudence Armstrong-Jones. Of *the* Armstrong-Joneses," she announced, with the emphasis on *the* denoting a name to be reckoned with.

"Ah, yes, *the* Armstrong-Joneses," I repeated, nodding knowingly. Although, I confess I had no knowledge of the name. "What is there you can tell me about her?" I asked.

"A spinster lady, is our Miss Armstrong-Jones," she stated, now seemingly more relaxed. "And likely to remain so if certain remarks made to me by my husband on previous occasions can be believed."

With the question arising as to whether the marriage would actually take place, I wondered if the woman was having second thoughts about her husband-to-be's overimbibing or indeed, his current financial situation. "Mr. Moore is without funds, is he?" I asked.

"He is without position," she answered. "But he does have a number of shares in the company so I would not call him destitute. Forgive me, dear lady," she suddenly announced, "but have we not crossed the boundary between gossip and information?''

"It's a fine line,'' I smiled. "Pray, continue.''

"Really, Mrs. Hudson, I do believe I had an easier time of it with Inspector MacDonald,'' she replied in mock admonishment. "That being said, I can only add it is generally assumed that our Mr. Moore will come into quite a tidy packet should the marriage take place.''

I left it at that.

During this momentary pause the lady of the house once more reached for her little silver answering bell and, holding it slightly aloft, gave it three quick shakes before replacing it on the desk. Within but a moment or two she had received a response. "Martin,'' she asked, addressing the butler, now framed within the open doorway, "has Dorothy arrived back as yet with Mrs. Birdie?''

"Not as yet, Mrs. Bramwell.''

"When she does, send her in straightaway to see me, would you?''

"Certainly, madam. Will that be all?''

"Yes, thank you, Martin. My daughter, Dorothy,'' she added, turning to me by way of explanation as the butler took his leave. "Nanny, Mrs. Birdie, that is, has taken her on a nice little visit to the zoo this afternoon.''

"Ah, yes,'' I smiled, leaning forward, "the papers did mention a daughter. How old a child would she be, Mrs. Bramwell?''

"Six, next May,'' she smiled. "And the flower of my heart, Mrs. Hudson,'' she added with a mother's pride.

"How is she taking the death of her father?" I asked.

"Better than I had expected, really. But then," she sighed, "we never really know what goes on inside their little heads, do we?"

Although not having been blessed with offspring of my own, being women, our conversation at that point turned in generalities to the problems of children and child-rearing until I at last brought the topic back to the issue at hand by asking what she could tell me of Roger Burke, the last of those present within the room on the night of her husband's murder.

"Ah, Roger," she exclaimed, with her face, at the mention of his name, breaking out into what I believed to be her first real smile of the day. "What a dear man he is. And jolly good fun, too. Though we never did see him as often as we would have liked. Quite the raconteur, Roger is. Invited to all the best parties."

"And this Roger Burke," I asked, "is he somehow connected to Bramwell Textile?"

"Heavens, no!" she giggled. "Roger's a member of the Royal Geographical Society. Seems he's always popping off to Africa for months at a time to discover something or other. That's where the two met—when my husband was on his one and only big game hunt. Poor Edgar," she sighed in remembrance, "picked up a touch of malaria, I'm afraid, and never went back."

"The Royal Geographical Society," I asked, "isn't that an explorer's club?"

"Indeed it is. Edgar was so taken with the adventure of it all he joined not long after his return to London. Both Roger and my husband remained friends ever since. And that,'' she said, ''completes the list. Is there anything else you wish to know?''

''Well, yes, actually there is,'' I replied rummaging through my purse for my spare note pad while mentally congratulating myself in having thought to bring an extra one along.

''And that would be—?'' she asked in a weary tone, on seeing me remove the pad, fold over the cover to the first page, and readjust myself in the chair.

I put it to her as pleasantly as I could that, notwithstanding her aversion to reliving the scene, I would have to know exactly what took place before, during, and after the fatal shot was fired.

''Yes, I thought you would,'' she answered with a resigned sigh before adding: ''Charades.''

''Pardon?''

''Charades,'' she repeated. ''We were all engaged in a game of charades in the drawing room, you see. Our chairs were set around in a sort of semi-circle while Edgar stood before us acting out his part. You do know how the game is played, don't you?''

''It's been a good many years,'' I answered. ''But I believe each player secretly writes down the name of a famous person or book or whatever on a slip of paper which is then folded over and dropped into a bowl. The one whose turn it is picks up one of the slips at random, reads it to himself, then acts it out in pantomime while the others try to guess who or what it is.''

''Yes,'' she said, ''that's it, exactly. And, as to our game, to the best of my recollection I believe we had just figured out it was the name of some famous composer we were after. I remember,'' she continued on, "that Roger, or perhaps it was David, made some sort of joke. We all began laughing except poor Edgar, who was becoming very frustrated with us. But in a good-natured way," she added. "And then—" She closed her eyes in the reliving of the moment and I could see that recalling the event was causing her no little stress.

"And then—?" I repeated, gently urging her on.

"Well, I don't know, really. I know it sounds bizarre, to say the least, but the next thing I saw," she continued with a slight tremor in her voice, "was my dear husband lying on the floor." At that point, she removed a handkerchief from under her sleeve to lightly dab her watery eyes. "There was a small red stain on the white of his shirt," she began, after a brief respite. "From it, a line of blood trickled its way down onto the rug from the wound in his chest." She buried her face in her hands and began to sob quietly.

I waited a moment then asked, "And you neither heard the shot nor saw the culprit?"

"I beg you, Mrs. Hudson, believe me, I saw and heard nothing."

This was utterly incredible. "And the murder weapon," I asked. "Is it true, as the papers say, that it's never been found?"

"Yes, all too true, I'm afraid."

"And the others," I continued, "they tell the same story, do they?"

"Indeed they do. And it goes without saying they are as completely bewildered by it all as I am. And," she added most emphatically, "just as innocent of the deed as myself."

At that point, I thanked my stars Vi was not present. "Well, somebody in the flamin' room must have shot him!" I could just imagine her exclaiming. As for myself, I could but shake my head in disbelief at the impossibility of it all. Saying nothing one way or the other, except to ask whether she knew of anyone who would have wished her husband dead, her reply was negative as I had imagined it would be. "And after you and the others became aware that something horrible had occurred, what happened then?" I asked.

She took a deep breath and plunged into a pool of information. "I remember," she began, "that I screamed, as did Patricia. Prudence, as I recall, just stood there, immobile, in a dazed condition. I saw Roger rush forward to where my husband lay sprawled on the floor, to lend what assistance he could. But it was to no avail. Edgar, it seems, had died instantly. By then, we women were becoming quite hysterical, I'm afraid. The men hurried us out into the hallway and into this very study. By that time, Martin had arrived on the scene and it was Arthur, I think, who told him to go immediately for the police. David, I was told, returned to the drawing room where my husband lay, closed the door, and stood guard outside until the police arrived. Please, Mrs. Hudson," she added softly, in quiet despair, "I'd rather not go on, if you don't mind. In any event, there's not much else I can tell you."

"That's quite all right," I assured her. "I understand perfectly how you must feel. I've just a few loose ends to tie up, then I'll be on my way."

"Loose ends?"

"I should like a list of your household staff," I

answered. "But perhaps I could see Martin about that, if you like."

"No, no," she replied, airily waving the idea aside. "I'm quite all right. In truth, we have but a small staff on hand unless, of course, we're entertaining a large dinner party. At which point, hired help is brought in."

"I see. So, as to your immediate staff, there is Martin, the butler . . ."

"Who also doubled as my husband's manservant and chauffeur."

"You own a automobile?" I blurted out, and immediately felt the fool for having asked. But, in all honesty, it was the first time I had ever met anyone who had ever owned one.

"Yes," she answered, seemingly unaware of my embarrassment. "But don't ask me the name of it. Smelly, noisy things that they are. Though quite beautiful to look at, I suppose. And men do so enjoy them, though lord knows why."

I nodded in acknowledgement of noisy automobiles before asking how long Martin had been in their employ.

"Two years," she said.

"I see. And as to the others—?"

"Well," she began, "there's Mrs. Smollett, our cook, a dear old soul who's been with us ever so long. Next on the list would be Rose. Rose Tuttle, our maid. Pretty little thing she is too. This is her third year with us, I believe. And then, of course, there's Nanny, that is to say, Mrs. Birdie, our child's governess. A wonderful woman, Mrs. Hudson. She and Dorothy get along famously together. I don't know what I'd do without her."

I offered up a smile before returning to a brief scanning of my notes. With my list being thus completed I informed Mrs. Bramwell that my next step would be to seek out all those who were present within the room for questioning.

"I can save you a little time there, Mrs. Hudson," she replied. "Inspector MacDonald has, to use his word, 'requested' a meeting here with those very people for tomorrow night at eight o'clock. It would be the perfect opportunity for you to come along as well. Although," she carried on, without so much as waiting for my reply, "why he deems it necessary is quite beyond me. What more can anyone say that hasn't been said already? You see," she added, tapping her finger on the desk to emphasize her point, "it's just as I told you. It's harrassment, pure and simple."

I could only state once again that the inspector would only be following police procedures. As to the meeting, I informed her it would suit my purposes ideally, "But, as to the time," I said, pursing my lips in thought, "you did say eight o'clock, didn't you?"

"Yes. Why," she asked, "is that not convenient for you?"

"Oh, yes, quite. Though to be perfectly honest, I was wondering if you could arrange for your guests to be here at seven. That way, I could have a little chat with each before the good inspector arrives."

"Certainly, Mrs. Hudson," she smiled. "I shall see to it they're notified of the change this afternoon."

"Most kind, I'm sure." Anything else I might have added was curtailed as the door was flung open and a little girl rushed in, followed in turn by a fairly large woman of some fifty-odd years with speckled gray hair, a warm smile, and eyes that twinkled behind little wire-rimmed spectacles that sat on the bridge of a pudgy nose. As for the child, she *was* a dear little thing. Indeed, the very miniature of her mother.

"Oh, mummy!" exclaimed the little girl on racing across the room, "we had ever so much fun. Didn't we, Nanny? We saw elephants and tigers and I threw peanuts at the monkeys and—"

"You simply must tell me all about it at dinner, Dorothy," chuckled her mother, rising from her chair and making her way round the desk. "Now come give me a nice big hug."

As she reached out to the child I couldn't help but notice a blue-black bruise on her left wrist. "Oh, Mrs. Bramwell," I exclaimed, "that does look quite nasty."

"What? Oh, that," she replied, with a tug to her sleeve in the act of covering it. "It's not as bad as it looks, actually. I'm always bumping into something or other, it seems. But where are my manners? Mrs. Birdie, Dorothy," she said, addressing the two, "this is Mrs. Hudson, who came to visit with me."

Visit? Yes, nicely put, I thought. After we had exchanged our hellos and pleasantries, there was a lull in the conversation which the child filled by stating, "My daddy's dead, you know."

It produced an awkward moment which ended with my stepping in to fill the breach by telling her that, yes, I did know and adding that I was sure he was having a very nice time of it up in heaven.

"I do so hope he's happy now," she answered very gravely for one so young.

"Yes, well, we mustn't keep Mrs. Hudson any longer," announced her mother. It was my cue to leave and I took it by saying my goodbyes to one and all with the added mention to the lady of the house that I would see her on the morrow.

"Until seven," she said.

"Until seven," I repeated.

Once outside, I paused on the top step, squared my shoulders, took a deep breath, and wondered what in the world I had gotten myself into.

TWO

Won't You Come into My
Parlor . . . ?

THE FOLLOWING DAY had passed quickly enough and, although I continued to blithely carry on with my usual household chores, I was hard pressed to keep my mind off the murder of Edgar Bramwell and those I intended to question that very night for I had thought it best not to allow myself to formulate any preconceived ideas before hearing what they had to say.

As for Vi, she had been in and out of the house during the better part of the day herself on various errands and it was not until we had a chance to sit down together for our evening meal that I had the opportunity to speak to her of my visit to Jane Bramwell. Now, with Vi knowing as much as I, we hurriedly cleared away the dishes and, after making ourselves presentable for our appointed meeting, donned coats and hats and stepped out into the night.

"Mr. Holmes has found his key then, has he?" queried Violet on closing the door behind us.

"No, not as yet," I answered. "Best leave it unlocked. He shouldn't be too long."

"Hmmph!" she sniffed. "Fine detective he is, I must say. Can't even find his own flamin' key."

With slivers of lightning crackling overhead and a splattering of rain heralding the approach of an upcoming storm, we thought ourselves fortunate to hail a cab before the deluge struck.

"Your tooth—it's still not hurting you, is it?" I asked as we continued to be jostled about this way and that as our driver pressed valiantly onward through sheets of windswept rain and pot-holed streets toward the Bramwell residence.

"It still feels a little queerlike at times," she confessed, clutching the door handle for safety's sake with one hand while giving a soft pat of comfort to her cheek with the other.

"At least," I stated with a reassuring smile, "you didn't have to have it pulled."

"Aye, but it's like I was telling you, if it were up to him I would have. I can fix it up for you now, he says, but by all accounts it should come out. As it is, he tells me, it won't last but a few years at best. A few years! I says. Well, at my age, I tells him, it'll be a race to see who goes first. Me or me tooth."

"Oh, Vi."

"No," she reiterated, "I told him I'd have none of it. Not even when he says he could hypnotize me so'd there'd be no pain."

"What's that you say? Hypnotize?"

"That's right. Put me into some kind of trance, he would, then pop it out without me so much as ever knowin' it happened. Well, I mean, can you imagine? There'd be me, in his chair, dead to the world like, and him, oily little man that he is, standing over me doing who knows what and me being none the wiser for it. No, I says, I'll have nowt to do with it, thank you very much. I've got me reputation to think of, I have," she added quite defensively. "If you know what I mean."

"I do indeed and I couldn't agree with you more," I stated in a show of female solidarity. "But, extraction by hypnosis, that *is* one for the books," I mused, more to myself than to Vi as we continued to be carried along at a good clip until at long last the mare thankfully slowed down to a walking gait. Knowing now it was only a matter of minutes before our arrival, I mentioned as much to Vi.

"I don't know if I'm looking forward to this here get together or not," she remarked on removing a small vanity mirror from her purse for a quick check of her hair.

"I know what you mean," I answered. "It's a queer state of affairs, at best."

"One good thing about it," she stated, "we won't have to ask them where they were at the time of the murder—what with them all being in the same ruddy room when it happened."

"Yes, but don't you see, that's what makes it so frustrating. There's no logic to it. The usual step-by-step procedures can't be implemented. I'm afraid we'll just simply have to play it by ear and hope for the best."

As the cabbie reined to a stop I turned to my old friend and, knowing her penchant for blurting out less than diplomatic utterances at the most inopportune time, I put it to her that it would best serve our purpose if she took on the task of writing down any pertinent facts that may arise during my questioning of those who awaited us within.

"Oh, I see," was her tart reply, "I'm to keep an open mind and a closed mouth, is that it?"

"No, nothing like that," I hastened to assure her. "It would simply look more professional, don't you see. Of course," I added, backing down somewhat in an attempt to mollify her, "if there's anything that puzzles you in regard to any answers given, feel free to ask away. But," I warned her, "bear in mind the last thing we want to do is turn this into some sort of interrogation. Think of it merely as a friendly little chat." I smiled. "Nothing more, nothing less."

"Easier to catch them off guard that way—is that what you're saying?"

"Exactly."

"You're too clever by half, you are, Emma Hudson. I'll say that for you."

After passing the amount of our fare plus tip (far less than my previous one but reasonable nonetheless) up through the hinged roof panel to our rain-bedraggled cabbie, we extricated ourselves forthwith and, splashing our feet through a pavement of puddles, made our way forward. Martin, who no doubt had heard the approach of our carriage, swung open the front door and bounded down the steps with umbrella at the ready and ushered us inside. It was not the most gracious of entrances but nonetheless we were glad to quit ourselves of coats and hats that, embarrassingly enough, dripped small splotches of water onto a highly polished floor.

As the Bramwell butler left to announce our arrival to the lady of the house, we caught the sounds of voices from somewhere within. "Sounds like they're already here," was Vi's comment accompanied by a nervous cough. "How's me hair?"

"Fine," I answered. "Mine?"

"Fine. You've brought pad and pencil then, did you?"

"Yes, of course I did," I stated, a little too sharply, I'm afraid.

"Well give it here then," she snapped, "if I'm to write down what they bloomin' well say."

It would seem our upcoming appearance before a roomful of murder suspects had made us both a trifle edgy.

"Good lookin' chap," was my companion's sudden and unexpected announcement whilst pocketing pad and pencil in her purse.

"Who?"

"The butler."

"Oh, Martin, yes," I nodded in agreement. "And quite an affable young man as well. As are all those with whom I've had the chance to speak."

"Queer, though, ain't it?"

"What?"

"I mean, what with everybody, as you say, being nice as pie like, where's the villain, eh? When you think that someone in this house put a bullet into poor Mr. Bramwell's chest, well, I ask you—"

"I see what you mean. But we've yet to meet the lot of them. In any event," I added with a smile, "I doubt if our murderer will turn out to be some half-crazed, one-eyed monster."

"It'd make it easier for us if he were. Know who we're up against then. Remember that Marcos bloke—the one with the bomb? Oh,'' she shuddered, ''he were a right good villain, he were, and no mistake. Why, I can remember—''

Thankfully, her remembrances were cut short by the arrival of Jane Bramwell looking both very somber and elegant in a mourning dress of black brocade and who, after my introduction of Violet and appropriate greetings all round, swept us along toward a closed door of stained oak. ''I've already mentioned to one and all,'' she informed us, pausing to rest her hand on the brass doorknob before entering, ''of your ladies acceptance in taking part in the investigation.''

''They're thrilled about that, I'm sure,'' muttered Vi, much to my chagrin.

We entered and were dutifully introduced to those assembled. And, as I was to find out before the evening was over, a many-faceted lot they were.

''Now then, Mrs. Hudson, just how do you intend to go about all this?'' questioned our hostess as all eyes turned as one in my direction.

''I thought perhaps,'' I began, after a nervous clearing of my throat, ''that it might be best if Mrs. Warner and I spoke to no more than one or two at a time. Privately,'' I added. ''Perhaps there's a room—?''

''Yes, of course. You can make use of the small anteroom, if you wish,'' she answered, indicating with a turn of her head a white-paneled door off to her left. ''If that's convenient.''

''I'm sure it will be just fine,'' I acknowledged, while noting suppressed smiles all round. But really, I ask you, who could blame them, seeing as they did two ladies of advanced years turning up out of nowhere, as it were, all set to solve a murder that, as yet, had left the best minds in Scotland Yard completely mystified. Nonetheless, I had promised to give it a go and give it a go I would, notwithstanding the more than ample fee previously agreed upon by the murdered man's wife. That being said, I now had to make a start somewhere. I looked questioningly about and for no particular reason singled out Bramwell's former general manager who stood, I noted, sullenly to the back of a seated Prudence Armstrong-Jones.

"Mr. Moore," I said pleasantly enough, "if you wouldn't mind—?" I let the sentence hang while indicating direction with a slight movement of my hand toward the aforementioned anteroom door.

His first response was to lean over his fiancée's chair and whisper something or other (I couldn't hear what) in her ear before at last making his way toward me. In a "ladies first" gesture, he waited until Violet and I had stepped through the doorway before following suit.

The room, with two straight-back cushioned chairs placed at the ends of a small table with the third off to one side, was perfect for my needs. While Vi made herself comfortable on the chair to my right, I took my place at one end of the table while the gentleman seated himself at the other.

Sitting now in close proximity to the man, my first impression was that his head, strangely enough, seemed too big for his body, as if it had been placed on those sloping shoulders by mistake. He was, I should say, no more than fifty. On his sallow face sat thick-glassed spectacles on the bridge of a red-veined nose. Below that nose a moustache badly in need of a trim covered the top half of a thin-lipped mouth. This was the brain behind Bramwell Textile? And yet . . . those eyes! Those deep, penetrating steel-blue eyes told a story that belied the face. For I sensed behind them dwelt both a highly perceptive and analytical mind. I had prejudged too quickly. This man was nobody's fool. It was also evident to me as he sat stiff-backed in his chair with arms folded defensively over his chest that we had before us, as the courts would say, a hostile witness.

"Let's begin then, shall we?" I said, conjuring up a smile in the hope it would be returned in kind from across the table. (It wasn't.) "Yes, well," I began again, "as to the night in question, what would you say, Mr. Moore, was the mood of those present, prior to the murder of the late Edgar Bramwell?"

I received no immediate response though he did seem genuinely surprised by the question.

"With respect to the general atmosphere within the room," I pressed on, restating the question, "do you recall sensing any underlying current of tension or anxiety in any one particular guest?"

"A good question," he at last answered while those eyes locked into mine for what seemed the longest time. "Not one that inspector chap has thought to ask as yet. Yes," he repeated with a wisp of a smile, "a good question, that."

So, the old gal is not quite the fool you first took her to be, is that it? It was a question I would have dearly loved to ask. I didn't. What I did do was nod politely. "And the answer?" I queried.

"The answer? No one that I saw was what you might call acting out of the ordinary. Though I'll admit I did find them to be a silly lot what with their games and all. I'm not into that sort of thing, you see. Though I suppose Pru—Miss Armstrong-Jones, that is, enjoys it well enough.''

"Games? Ah, yes, the game of charades that was played that night, you mean.''

"Yes, quite. Had to guess the name of some such famous book or other, as I recall. Stuff and nonsense, I say,'' he snorted. "What do I know of books? I'm a businessman. Facts and figures, that's my ticket. Books!'' Another snort. "Ledgers now, that would be a different matter.''

"Don't know if I've ever heard of any famous ledgers,'' remarked Vi with a saucy wink in my direction.

I could have killed her.

"Eh, what's that?'' he snapped.

"Tell me,'' I spoke up, quickly interceding in an attempt to set things back on course, "if I'm not mistaken (and I knew I wasn't) it was during the game of charades that the murder occurred, was it not?''

"It was,'' he acknowledged with a slight nod. "I can tell you that much, at least. But no doubt your interest lies in what happened just prior to the murder.''

I, in turn, answered with a nod.

"I'm afraid,'' he began, "all I can tell you is what I've already told the inspector on more than one occasion, and that is, the first indication I had that something was amiss was on hearing Mrs. MacPhail scream. I immediately turned in her direction and, I tell you quite frankly, Mrs. Hudson, I shall never forget the look of utter horror I saw on that woman's face as she stood with one hand cupped over her mouth while the other pointed to the body on the floor. Even with his bloodied shirt I confess it took me a moment or two to realize young Bramwell had been shot.''

"But, Mr. Moore, surely you must have seen—''

"I tell you, madam,'' he interjected quite forcefully, ''that is the extent of it! Do you not think,'' he continued on in a now less abrasive tone, ''that I would rather be in a position to tell the tale of some crazed chap or other I saw race into the room, do the deed, and race back out? Unfortunately, I cannot. Would that I could, ladies. Would that I could. This whole affair,'' he added quite despairingly, ''has made us all look like complete fools.''

"Could there have been someone in the room hiding behind a chair, like?'' ventured Vi.

He shook his head. ''You've seen the room. There's no place one could hide. Besides, we were all moving about—someone would have spotted the beggar.''

"And you heard no shot?'' I asked.

"Not a sound,'' he answered quietly with a resigned sigh.

After a momentary silence, the gentleman asked me if I would be conferring with the inspector on his arrival.

"Yes, of course,'' I answered. ''Why'd you ask?''

"I should like it to be noted,'' he stated in measured tone, ''that I have readily made myself available to you and have cooperated in any way I could in regard to this horrendous situation the lady now finds herself in.''

"The lady?''

"Why, Mrs. Bramwell, of course," he answered simply.

I confess I was left slightly bewildered. "Am I to take it that you're saying, in effect, that you believe Mrs. Bramwell is, in some way, responsible for her husband's murder?"

"That is not what I said," he was quick to reply. "I am merely stating that she is the murdered man's wife and the murder did occur in her home."

"Oh, I see," Vi spoke up, "and if some bloke or other robbed a bank you'd blame the manager then, would you?"

He eyed her coolly but made no reply.

"But surely you must realize, Mr. Moore," I said, "that everyone in the room that night is suspect, yourself included."

"And surely *you* must realize," he answered in what I can only describe as a slightly sardonic tone, "that in order for me to be taken seriously by the police as a suspect, I would have to have had a motive."

"Then you don't consider the fact," I answered, mindful to pick my words as carefully as I would stepping-stones across a stream, "that your ah, untimely dismissal from Bramwell Textile would constitute—"

"My untimely dismissal, as you put it," he interjected quite sharply, "was nothing more than a leave of absence. If you knew anything about the business world, madam, and it appears to me that you do not," he continued on in a most belligerent manner, "you would know that men of business do not go about shooting their employers simply because they've been given the sack. If that, indeed, is what you're implying." With that, he settled back in his chair with arms refolded over his chest feeling quite satisfied with himself, I'm sure.

Oh, dear, I groaned inwardly, this wasn't going well at all. It seemed the nice little chat I had envisaged had become more confrontational than conversational. So be it. Perhaps it was time for a little less pussyfooting from my side of the table.

"Mr. Moore," I stated in a manner calm and collected, "I'm going to tell you what I *do* know. After which, you may respond as you see fit. Now, then," I began, "as to an employee shooting his employer because he believes he has been wrongfully dismissed, while highly improbable, is still within the realm of possibility. However, I believe your particular situation goes much deeper than that. According to information made available to me, Mr. Bramwell had no other recourse than to relieve you of your duties not only with respect to the continuing loss of profit the company was experiencing under your directorship but to your, shall we say, alcoholic indulgences as well. Ergo, you find yourself without a position. You are also, I would imagine, finding yourself being ostracized by members of your club as well as various gentlemen of industry as gossip filters round as to the real reason for the relinquishing of your position from Bramwell. We now add to that," I continued on at a quickening pace in an effort to stave off a probable broadside of rebuttals, "the matter of your upcoming marriage and whether, in fact, it will take place at all. Aside from any affection you feel for Miss Armstrong-Jones, the fact that the family is one of wealth would, in itself, generate a needed source of revenue for you. To sum up, in a matter of weeks you have found yourself not only unemployed but on shaky ground with respect to your forthcoming marriage. No doubt you would say the fault lies not with yourself but with one person and one person only—the murdered man, Edgar Bramwell. Mind you,'' I was quick to add, "that is not to say you are the guilty party, only that motive is there."

That being said, I sat back and mentally steeled myself for a shower of denouncements I felt sure would now rain down upon me. Strangely enough, he said nothing. The face was immobile. Only the eyes continued to bore into mine.

"Who told you all this?" he spoke at last while continuing to study me closely from across the table.

"I'm sorry," I answered, "that is privileged information."

"Is it indeed?" The voice was contemptuous. "I put it to you, madam, that what you have been told is a fanciful tale at best. Based on nothing more than half-truths and conjecture."

So saying, he rose brusquely from his chair and strode with purposeful strides across the floor, pausing only at the door to wish us a curt "good night" before exiting the room.

"I should hope they're not all like him," stated Vi with a rueful shake of her head. "Who's next, then?"

Prudence Armstrong-Jones was a plain-faced woman whose eyes, set a little too close to the bridge of her nose, did nothing to enhance the features of a woman I judged to be in her mid-forties. Surrounding the oval face, wisps of gray could be seen within the mousey-brown yet elaborately upswept hair with its row of tiny ringlets framing the forehead. It was a style I believed best left to a woman half her age.

"Whatever did you say to poor Arthur?" she asked on taking the chair vacated only moments before by her intended.

"Nothing that didn't need to be said," I answered. "However, if he appeared out of sorts it's understandable, given the strain he's been under of late."

"Yes, this murder business," she sympathized. "Terrible. Just terrible."

"I speak of your upcoming marriage as well," I replied.

"My marriage?" was the startled response. "I would hardly have thought my marriage to be a topic of conversation. I was under the impression you wished to speak to us in regard to the murder."

"Aye, that's right, we do," spoke Vi. "Leastways, Mrs. Hudson here does," she added with a spurious glance in my direction.

It would appear that Vi, feeling she'd been relegated to the role of a mere note-taker, was feeling a trifle out of sorts herself with yours truly. The woman acknowledged Violet's comment with a slight nod of her head before turning her attention back to me. As she did, I announced that I was going to be quite candid with her as I hoped she'd be with me.

"Yes, go on, then," she answered, eyeing me, understandably I thought, a trifle apprehensively.

"From the information we've been given," I began, "and I might add, it was not from Mr. Moore, I, that is to say, Mrs. Warner and I," I added as a compensating gesture to my companion, "are under the impression that there could very well be a cancellation of your wedding plans. Are you, yourself, having second thoughts?"

"I?" was her surprised reaction. "No, not at all. Though, as I say, I fail to see what my private life has to do with Mr. Bramwell's murder. But, if you must know, it's my father, you see. The dear soul is getting on in years and, since I am his only child, he would of course like to see me married. The thing of it is, father is not, shall we say, all that keen in bestowing his blessing on the marriage."

"And the reason being—?" I asked.

"Yes, well, without putting too fine a point on it," she hedged, "Mr. Moore has fallen on hard times of late and father would rather I, well—"

"Find yourself a more suitable mate, is that it?" asked Vi on looking up from her notes.

"Yes, I suppose so," she answered after a prolonged and plaintive sigh. "If there *are* more fish in the sea, as father so often reminds me," she added, "they no longer swim in my direction. And why should they? Good, heavens, ladies," she suddenly blurted out, "I'm nearly forty years old!"

Nearly, forty? Ah, well, I thought, suppressing a smile, a woman's preogative. We're all guilty of it, I suppose. Vi, in turn, stifled an odd little noise in her throat with a fake cough or two and fortunately said nothing.

"Yes, I would imagine it doesn't get any easier for single ladies in this day and age," was the response I finally managed to come up with. "And Mr. Moore's reaction to all this?" I asked. "In regard to the postponement of your marriage, I mean."

"Why," she answered with a smile, "lovely man that he is, it's his wish to wait till father comes round to the idea. Doesn't want to be the cause of a rift, he says, between father and daughter."

Go ahead Vi, say it, I thought, no blessing—no money. Fortunately, she was so engrossed in her writing the implication of what she had heard escaped her. As for Miss Armstrong-Jones, she again raised the question as to why plans for her marriage would be of concern to us. "Just routine questioning," I assured her and let it go at that. I then pressed on by asking if she could clear up for us the reason why she and Mr. Moore decided to attend the party.

"To be honest with you, Mrs. Hudson," she replied, "I would rather have passed on it. But Jane—Mrs. Bramwell, is such a dear and she does so love giving parties, we couldn't refuse her invitation. Besides," she added, "Arthur thought an opportunity might arise to speak privately to Edgar about..." she paused. "About certain things."

"His reinstatement with the company, you mean."

"Oh!" was the lady's surprised reaction. "You know about that?"

I nodded that I did and, with respect to the following question I put to her as to what she could tell us of the night in question, we were told no more than what we already knew. She had heard no shot. She had seen no one commit the deed.

"But surely, dear lady," I stated with no small measure of frustration, "over the intervening days, you must have given some thought as to what actually happened or, for that matter, who it was that was actually responsible for the crime."

"Yes, Mrs. Hudson," she answered very solemnly, "I have indeed given it some thought. In truth, it has never left my mind. We have all been genuinely upset by it as well you can imagine. None more so than Mr. Moore and myself."

"And you suspect no one?"

"Well . . ." She hesitated and, with downcast eyes, toyed with the folds in her dress, playing for time it would seem, while wondering, no doubt, whether to voice her opinion aloud.

"Yes, go on," I urged. "You suspect—?"

"Mr. Bramwell," she announced.

I was left utterly bewildered, as indeed, was Vi. "Mr. Bramwell?" I repeated, wondering whether I had heard her correctly.

"Yes," she answered. "It's a theory I have, you see. And Arthur thinks it might jolly well be the answer."

"Then, in effect, what you are saying," I stated, "is that Edgar Bramwell committed suicide."

"Took his own life, yes," she replied, seemingly quite satisfied with herself.

"Oh, yes?" sang out Vi. "And just how did he do that, then? What with him standing there in the middle of the room and everyone gawking at him, like?"

I leaned forward in my chair anxiously awaiting the woman's reply. Could this, I thought, be the first turn of the key to unlocking the riddle?

"I haven't the foggiest," she answered.

"What! You haven't the foggiest?" I repeated incredulously. "Then why on earth did you say you believe he did away with himself?"

"For the simple reason, Mrs. Hudson," she stated

quite matter-of-factly, "that I simply refuse to believe that anyone in the room that night could have done anything so horrid."

Vi and I exchanged despairing glances.

"Yes, well, thank you ever so much, Miss Armstrong-Jones, for your time," I said on rising to my feet. "We shan't keep you any longer."

As Vi and I escorted her to the door she paused long enough to ask whether she should make known her theory to the inspector.

"Why, yes, 'course you should," answered Vi, straight-of-face. "Got the makings of a Sherlock Holmes, you have."

"Do you really think so?" she gushed. "Oh, I can't wait to tell Arthur."

"Just one more thing, Miss Armstrong-Jones," I said. "A favor, if you will."

"Yes?"

"Would you mind asking Mr. and Mrs. MacPhail to step in next?"

"Yes, certainly, Mrs. Hudson."

No sooner had the lady departed than I whirled on my companion. "Mrs. Warner," I exclaimed in mock seriousness, "how could you? The makings of a Sherlock Holmes—really!"

"Well, it gave her a bit of a lift, like," she answered with a wink. "So where's the harm in it, eh? But, as to this suicide business of hers," she added, "I mean—can you imagine?"

"You know, now that I think about it," I answered in thoughtful reply, "given the fact that at this point in time we have absolutely no idea of what *did* happen, I suppose even *that* is possible."

*   *   *

"Oh, I'm so sorry, Mr. MacPhail," I apologized as the gentleman and his wife made their entrance. "I had forgotten we lack a fourth chair. Perhaps I should see if I can get another from Mrs. Bramwell."

"Not too worry, Mrs. Hudson. I'll stand here behind Patricia, if that's all right," he answered with a smile as his wife eased herself into the chair opposite me.

"Whatever suits you best," I replied, returning the smile. "I daresay we shan't keep you too long in any event."

From his stance in back of his wife, he lightly placed a hand on her shoulder in a gesture of reassurance, removing it only occasionally to fling back an unruly lock of sandy-brown hair that persisted in having its way by continually flopping down over his forehead. His face I found to be thoughtful and intelligent and the ruddy complexion, which I attributed to a tropic sun, was only now relinquishing itself to its original and more familiar London pallor. He was, I should say, a man in his early thirties, small and compact with the look of the athlete about him.

As for his wife, Patricia MacPhail was still a quite pretty young thing. I say "still," for although she would be only a year or two younger than her husband, I could see within those features what once would have been a strikingly beautiful woman. But equatorial climes are not always kind to women of northern hemispheres. And though I could picture her never straying too far afoot from the confines of a shaded verandah without parasol in hand, years under an Asian sun had taken its toll. The corn-yellow hair was without sheen and the cheeks over-rouged to compensate for the dryness of the skin. Even now, telltale lines could be seen around the corners of the pale blue eyes and full-lipped mouth.

"I understand you and your wife have only recently arrived back from the Far East, Mr. Mac-Phail," I said, by way of opening up the conversation.

"Yes, quite right," he responded. "We've been back now a little over two weeks, I should say."

"From—?"

"Indonesia, actually. I've a rubber plantation there."

"It's our first trip back in I don't know how many years," added his wife.

"I believe about five," I replied.

The young lady appeared quite taken aback. "Why, yes, it is," she answered. "However did you know?"

In lieu of an answer I offered up what I hoped was an enigmatic smile. I had no wish to embarrass the woman by revealing the answer lay in the style of her apparel.

"It's the cut of your dress, see," announced Vi, who evidently had no such qualms. "It's not the style they're wearin' nowadays. We're quick to spot things like that, being detectives and all. Isn't that right, Em—Mrs. Hudson."

I cast her a withering glare. "Quite—right, Mrs. Warner," I replied in the iciest of tones.

Vi, catching sight of the woman's flushed cheeks, realized her *faux pas* and rather than end it there, continued to babble on. "That's not to say you don't look very nice, luv. Yes, very nice indeed, I must

say. Turned out far better, you are, than some of the
women you see now. Why, I was saying to Mrs.
Hudson, just the other day—''

''Ah, Mrs. Warner,'' said I, stepping in on seeing
she had no ending to her story, ''if your pencil is
worn down, I do have another in my purse.'' This
was the only thing I could think of to say at the
moment.

''What? Oh, I see,'' she replied, catching my eye
as well as my drift. ''No, it'll do for now. I just dab
it to my tongue every so often like.''

''Fine. Fine. Now then, Mr. MacPhail,'' I said,
anxious to swing us back on course, ''I believe that
you were friends for a number of years with the late
Edgar Bramwell, were you not?''

''Yes,'' he answered. ''Ever since our dear old
days at Oxford, actually. As I recall, Edgar was more
the scholarly type than ever I was. I'm afraid in
those days I was much more interested in soccer than
Socrates. Still am,'' he smiled. ''But for all that, we
did remain friends of a sort. In fact,'' he added with
a wry smile, ''I was about the only friend he had
there.''

''Oh,'' I asked, ''why was that?''

''He had a devil of a temper, you see. Though it
never bothered me as it did some of the other chaps.
The trick was never to take him seriously.''

This, I thought, was going much better than had
our two previous sessions. Such an open and coop-
erative young man. ''And after Oxford,'' I asked, ''I
take it you continued to socialize?''

''Yes,'' he answered, ''to a certain extent. We had
taken flats not far from each other here in London.
This would be just around the time I had met

Patricia. In fact, every now and then, the three of us would go out on the town, as they say. We did have some high old times together, didn't we, dear?'' he asked, with a loving pat to her shoulder.

''What? Oh, oh, yes,'' she stammered, as if lost deep in thought.

''About this here rubber plantation of yours,'' Vi sang out quite unexpectedly, no doubt believing she'd been silent much too long, ''how does it grow, eh?''

''Grow?'' questioned the man. ''The rubber, you mean?''

''Aye. Doubt if it grows on trees,'' said she, smiling to herself at the thought of it.

''To be perfectly honest with you, Mrs. Warner,'' he answered, ''I suppose you could say that it does.''

''Oh, yes, I'm sure,'' she chuckled, feeling, no doubt, the gentleman was putting her on. ''Pick them off the branches like apples, do you? Little rubber balls, are they?''

I looked embarrassed. Mrs. MacPhail smiled. Mr. MacPhail laughed.

''No,'' he said, ''it's not quite like that. We process the leaves. Actually, it's a rubber tree plant. *Hevea brasilieusis*, if you care for its Latin name.''

''Can't say that I do,'' admitted Violet returning to her notes, while no doubt castigating herself for having spoken of it in the first place.

As for myself, I found it fortunate that she had, for it provided me the opportunity to lead into a question or two I had regarding that self-same subject. ''From what I read in the papers, Mr. Mac-Phail,'' I said, thankful for my nightly habit of devouring the *Times* from front to back over a nice hot cup of tea, "I understand the Asian rubber market is on quite a downslide."

"Yes, it's true," he ruefully admitted, flicking back a lock of hair. "The industry, I'm sorry to say, has in large part shifted to South America. Time and transportation costs being the main factor. By the time a cargo of Asian rubber is rounding the cape, shipments from Brazil are already docking in European ports. Combine that," he went on, "with the two bad years we've just gone through with an above average rainfall and, well—"

"My dear Mr. MacPhail," I remarked, more distressed than surprised, "are you saying then that you're financially ruined?"

"Except for a small inheritance that I have," he admitted.

"But can you not apply to your bank for a loan to see you through?"

"Don't think David hasn't tried," answered his wife with a wan smile. "The Asian market's too much of a risk factor, they say."

"But there's still money to be made out there," added her husband most convincingly. "We haven't lost the market, we're simply sharing it now, don't you see?"

"Yes, I see," I answered. "But from what you say, obviously the banks don't."

"Chucked the whole business then, have you?" asked Vi, while in the process of dabbing pencil tip to tongue. "That's why you two came back, is it?"

"I would imagine, Mrs. Warner," I spoke up before an answer could be given from either one of the two, "that the reason for their arrival here in London was in order for the gentleman to seek a personal loan from an old school chum, was it not?'' I asked, turning my attention back to the man.

''Yes, you're quite right,'' he answered. ''It's no secret. I sought out Edgar to negotiate a business loan. It's as simple as that.''

''But he turned you down,'' I said knowingly, though I had no idea one way or the other.

''True,'' he admitted after a thoughtful pause.

''Unfortunate,'' I commiserated, ''but understandable given the fact that Bramwell's not all that solvent itself.''

''Balderdash!'' The word exploded out of him, quite startling me. ''I've done some checking on my own, Mrs. Hudson, and it might interest you to know that all this business about Mr. Moore's drinking and lack of stewardship was just a ploy on Edgar's part to have the board of directors ease him out so that he might have his own man brought in. Bramwell's profits are down,'' he admitted, ''but the company is hardly on the verge of bankruptcy.''

''Then why should he turn you down?'' I asked, and, as I did, I saw his fingers tense and tighten on his wife's shoulders. As for the woman herself, she sat with lowered eyes and said nothing.

''I don't know,'' was all he said.

As to what they could tell me of the crime, it was no more than what we had heard from those we had spoken to previously.

''It was you, Mrs. MacPhail,'' I asked, ''who first spotted the body of Edgar Bramwell on the floor, was it not?''

''Yes,'' she acknowledged. ''I'm afraid I let out quite a dreadful scream on seeing him lying there like that—all bloody and, oh,'' she shuddered, ''it was just horrible.''

''And you saw nothing before that? Not so much as an instant before?''

She shook her head. ''No,'' she answered. ''One minute he was standing there and the next—''

''I know it must sound as if we're hiding something, Mrs. Hudson,'' interjected her husband, ''but I assure you, we're not.''

''Hmmm,'' was my noncommital reply.

''Might I be so bold as to make a suggestion?'' queried Vi, resting pad and pencil on her lap. ''If nobody seems to know or remember what were going on right under their noses like, perhaps you were all, you know—'' She cupped her hand and raised it pantomime fashion to her mouth.

''What? Drinking, you mean? No, I'm afraid not,'' smiled the man. ''My wife and I are social drinkers, at best. As for the rest, I don't recall seeing anyone in what you would call a state of intoxication. Though, I suppose our African explorer friend did have a bit of a glow on,'' he admitted with a smile.

''We were much too busy having ever so much fun playing charades,'' added his wife.

I had no idea what to make of what I had heard and, though by now I was aware of what the answer to my next question would be, I put it forward more as a formality if nothing else. ''Were you aware, Mr. MacPhail,'' I asked, ''of hearing the sound of a pistol shot from within the room?''

''I'm sorry to say,'' he replied, ''I didn't hear a blessed thing.''

Needless to say his answer didn't surprise me.

"And you, Mrs. MacPhail?" I asked off-handedly.

"I'm—I'm not sure," she answered hesitantly.

"What!" I pounced on her words. "How'd you mean—not sure?"

"Well," she responded slowly, biting her lower lip in thought, "perhaps I did."

"Why, Pat, what's all this!" exclaimed her husband. "You never mentioned anything about this before to me."

"I've had time to think about it. To go over it in my mind," she answered.

"Yes," I said leaning forward in my chair, "and you believe you heard—what? A shot?"

"No," she answered, "that would be a loud bang, wouldn't it? The only way I can explain it is by saying it sounded like a muffled thud, as if heard from a long way off. But that sounds silly, doesn't it?" she added with a deprecating smile.

"Perhaps you only dreamed you heard something," suggested her husband. "This whole wretched affair has been a great strain on her, Mrs. Hudson," he added. "As, I'll admit, it has been on myself as well."

"Yes, I can understand that it would. But you did hear something, Mrs. MacPhail," I asked, returning my attention back to the woman. "Yes?"

"Yes," she answered at last. "I believe I did."

"And is that significant?" asked her husband.

"It could very well be," I answered, looking very wise. "It could very well be." Whether it actually could be or not only time would tell. But the fact that she had heard *something* was, in itself, food for thought.

"One last question, if you please," I said by way

of bringing our little session to an end. "As neither of you can offer up an explanation as to how the murder was committed, have you, yourselves, any thought as to who might be the guilty party? Mrs. MacPhail? Mind you," I was quick to add, "whatever you say will of course be kept strictly confidential."

The young lady who, by this time, had risen to her feet, answered that she had no idea whatsoever.

"And you, Mr. MacPhail?"

"The only one who comes to mind," he answered with a thoughtful rub or two to his chin, "would be that African explorer chap, Burke. For the only reason I suppose is that one tends to associate guns, shooting, and that sort of thing with someone in his profession. If indeed," he added, "someone in the room that night actually did do it."

"How could it be otherwise?" I asked.

As the MacPhails left, in stepped Roger Burke, a big, hearty man no more than forty, I would imagine, complete with a magnificent bushy-red beard and a presence that seemed to engulf the room. As he took his chair opposite me I couldn't help but note that, while properly dressed, he looked slightly uncomfortable in his evening attire, running his fingers as he did every so often round the inside of his starched collar as if to ease the feeling of being slowly strangled to death.

As I sat there in silent sympathy for him wondering how to begin, the gentleman himself took the initiative.

"Now why is it I would suddenly think of that old nursery rhyme—won't you come into my parlor, said the spider to the fly?'' he asked, with a wicked little grin.

"Spiders, are we?'' responded Vi just as mischievously. "It would take a right good web to catch you if we were. Besides,'' she added, sizing up the strapping six-footer, "you don't look like any fly I've ever laid me eyes on.''

He threw back his head, emitting a deep, raucous laugh.

"Perhaps you could tell us something about yourself, Mr. Burke,'' I said when the laughter had subsided.

"Myself? Not the murder?''

"Plenty of time for that,'' I answered.

"Quite. Right, then. I, madam,'' he intoned, "am the last of the great African explorers. I follow, belatedly mind you, in the footsteps of such men as Burton, Speke, Baker, Livingstone, and the rest of those intrepid souls who made the dark continent a little lighter for the white man.''

"Oh, it all sounds so exciting,'' gushed Violet.

"Yes, doesn't it,'' he said. "Admittedly though,'' he added, "I may have laid it on a bit thick. Unfortunately, there are no new Niles of which to seek their source and the continent itself, for all intents and purposes, has been fairly well mapped. Born a good seventy years too late, that's my problem. As a member of the Royal Geographical Society I am left to collect and catalogue various forms of flora and fauna, seek out the tributaries of the odd river as yet unmapped and, to add to my own personal coffers, escort rich Englishmen out on safaris.''

"As you did with Mr. Bramwell,'' I said.

"Quite right, Mrs. Hudson. Though it was not one

of our better ones, I'm afraid. The silly beggar came down with a bad case of malaria and what quinine we had on hand didn't seem to help all that much. After having Edgar, half-mad with fever, strapped to a litter, our party backtracked its way to the coast where a ship bound for Cairo got him to the hospital just in time. From there, it was back to England for dear old Edgar."

"Why," exclaimed Violet, "you saved his life, you did!"

"Yes, didn't I."

"He was a member of the society as well, wasn't he?" I asked.

"After recuperating in London he put his name forward for membership. Evidently his bout with malaria hadn't dampened his enthusiasm for the continent. But between you and me," he added with yet another tug to his collar, "I understand he donated quite a sizeable sum to the RGS. Bought his way in, you might say. But in answer to your question, yes, we were both members. In fact," he went on with no prodding from me, "it was at the society that I approached him with the idea of financing an expedition to the land of the Masai."

"An expedition? For what purpose, Mr. Burke?"

"I have in my possession, madam," he answered, leaning forward with lowered voice, "an ancient map outlining the location of a lost diamond mine. Diamonds! Can you imagine!" he sang out, completely forgetting his conspiratorial tone. "Why, who knows, it might even rival South Africa in output."

"How in the world did you come by such a map?" I asked.

"Ah, an interesting story in itself, that," he smiled. "Suffice it to say, an old Arab slave dealer in Gondokoro who I had once befriended gave it to me on his death bed."

"And this land of the Masai," I questioned. "Where is that?"

"East Africa," he answered guardedly. "That's all I can tell you."

"Don't worry, your secret's safe with us, luv," Vi was quick to assure him. "What Mrs. Hudson and I know about Africa you could put in a thimble."

He responded with a light-hearted chuckle. My reaction was to question him as to why he did not seek financing from the Royal Geographical Society.

"I did!" was the angry response. "They turned me down. Idiots. They tell me there are no diamonds to be found in that region. As for the map? A fake, they say. Old men who have never ventured closer to the wild than the London Zoo tell me what is and what is not in Africa! I'm sorry," he apologized, sinking back in his chair. "I didn't mean to get so carried away."

"Perfectly understandable, I'm sure. And as for Edgar Bramwell's part in all this?" I asked.

"Good old Edgar," he beamed. "He agreed at once to put up the necessary money. Unfortunately, the man met his end before we could actually formalize it all."

"And how did he meet his end?" I asked, straight out.

"How?" I received a most puzzling look. "Why," he answered, "he was shot."

"Well, we know *that*," interjected an exasperated Vi. "The question is, how?"

"Ah, well, as to that, dear ladies," he answered, "I'm as completely in the dark as, no doubt, you are yourselves."

"Even though you were in the room when it happened," I stated.

"Even though," he admitted.

"And you have no idea," I carried on, "as to how the murder could have been carried out?"

"None whatsoever, I'm afraid. But whoever it was must have been an extremely clever fellow. I'll grant him that much."

"And this extremely clever fellow," I pressed on. "Do you have any thoughts as to who he might be?"

"Hmmm—no, not really."

"But you do have an idea or two, I take it?"

"Look here, Mrs. Hudson," he announced after a prolonged pause, "I'm not one for pointing fingers, mind you, but being the oddity I am, one does get invited to all sorts of social gatherings and one does hear all sorts of gossip."

"And what does 'one' hear?" questioned Vi.

"I take it you ladies have heard that the Mac-Phails and Bramwell used to chum around together at one time?"

"Yes," I said, "we're aware of that."

"Oh," he seemed surprised. "Well then, no doubt you heard about the night MacPhail caught Bramwell making advances, as they say, toward his wife shortly before they were to be married."

"No, I didn't," I dutifully admitted. But it would explain, I thought, the certain tenseness they had exhibited when I questioned the young man as to why Edgar Bramwell had turned down his request for a loan.

"Oh, yes," he continued on, "it was quite a donnybrook from what they tell me, with Edgar getting the worst of it. They did manage to patch things up in the long run but it was never the same between them, from what I understand."

"Then, what you are offering up, Mr. Burke," I said, "is a motive for—"

"What I am offering up, Mrs. Hudson," said he, stepping in, "is gossip. Make of it what you will. If you know London society, you know it's the lifeblood of their existence. Is it any wonder," he added with a weary smile, "that I long for the peace and quiet of the African plain?"

With the interview at an end we vacated the anteroom and rejoined the assembly with Mr. Burke, who, on eyeing the whiskey decanter on the far table, excused himself from our presence. On seeing us enter, Jane Bramwell broke off a conversation with Patricia MacPhail and quickly approached.

"You simply must tell me everything they said," she whispered, drawing us aside.

"Certainly, Mrs. Bramwell," I answered as tactfully as I could. "I'll be in touch with you just as soon as Mrs. Warner and I have had a chance to go over our notes."

"Oh, yes, yes of course," she answered, masking her disappointment with an understanding smile. "That would be best, wouldn't it? Oh, by the way," she added, "Inspector MacDonald has just recently joined us. On my mentioning your involvement in all this he asked if he might have a word or two with you. That's him over there," she said, indicating with a turn of her head a portly gentleman none too elegantly attired in a rumpled brown tweed suit with shoes, black, unpolished, and slightly run down at the heels. "Come along," she said, "I'll introduce you two."

"If I'm not mistaken, you're the same Mrs. Hudson in whose house lodges the famous Sherlock Holmes, are you not?" he asked after the lady of the house had made her introductions.

I acknowledged as much with a slight nod of my head, having long since resigned myself to the fact that I would always be known as such.

"And Mrs. Warner," he continued on, "you are—?"

"Her partner in crime, you might say," answered Vi with a chuckle.

"And companion," I added.

"Yes, we've heard of you ladies down at the Yard, actually. Talk does get around you know," he smiled. "And Mrs. Bramwell here has brought you in to solve this murder for us, has she?" The smile remained but I detected a sliver of sarcasm slipping in.

"Our purpose is to help in any way we can," I answered simply.

"I see. Ah, Mrs. Bramwell, I wonder if you'd excuse us for a minute or two?" he asked pleasantly enough.

"Yes, certainly, Inspector," she answered. "If I don't see you later on, Mrs. Hudson," she added, returning her attention to me, "I'll send word as to a date for our next meeting."

As the young lady took her leave, the inspector's

mood abruptly changed. "Right. What's all this then, eh?" he snapped.

"All—this?" I repeated, startled by his sudden and unexpected outburst of hostility.

"Muckin' about in police business," was the grim reply.

"Inspector MacDonald," I announced defensively, "as I say, we have been engaged by Mrs. Bramwell to help in any way we could to solve the murder of her husband. Now, if by so doing we've broken some law—"

"You've broken no law," he stated, mindful to keep his voice below conversational level. "And more's the pity for that, I say. This is police work, madam. It's not a job fit for a civilian," he added, spitting out the word "civilian" as if it had left a bad taste in his mouth.

Vi had her own snide comment to make. "Oh I see," she said, "Scotland Yard has it pretty well all solved then have they?"

"We hope to have very shortly, as a matter of fact, Mrs. Warner," he announced all too smugly. "It's really not as baffling as the papers would have you believe."

"Is it not?" I asked rather skeptically.

"If you'd been on the force as long as I have, Mrs. Hudson, you'd see through this 'invisible man' nonsense in jig time. Oh, yes," he continued on, feeling quite full of himself, "it's really no mystery. One person commits the murder and the rest bond together behind him professing no knowledge of the crime whatsoever. It's as simple as that."

"Not quite," I answered.

"Eh, what's that?"

"Inspector MacDonald," I stated, "I have just finished questioning the lot of them and, while it's true no one has admitted any involvement in the crime, each one intimates, in one way or another, someone they suspect might be the guilty party. I found no bonding together, as you put it."

"So much for your theory, eh, Inspector?" chided Vi.

"Not really," he answered, after a moment's pause. "The circle is beginning to crack, don't you see. They're beginning to turn on each other—like a pack of wolves," he added, a little over-dramatically I thought. For all that, I found it hard to believe his hypothesis of it being simply a case of cover-up by all parties concerned and mentioned as much to him.

"Time will tell, Mrs. Hudson," he replied all too knowingly. "Time will tell."

"It will indeed, Inspector," I answered. "It will indeed."

THREE

Presenting Peter Wooley

⟲ THE FOLLOWING MORNING found me up bright and early for I had much to do and much to occupy my mind. First on the agenda was a trip to the greengrocers for I had noted that we were running low on food and, although we were a household of detectives (to a more or lesser degree), even detectives have to eat.

And so it was by noon of that same morning, having acquired the necessary items, I found myself threading my way home along Baker Street laden with an armful of grocery bags that seemed to take on added weight with every step I took. I therefore thought myself quite fortunate in spotting Mr. Wooley taking in the sun on the front stoop of his lodgings. Although I only knew the man to say hello from having met him once or twice when he entertained the children with his magic act at our local church picnics or Christmas parties, I felt comfortable enough to stop and chat and, in the process, afford myself a brief respite.

"And how is Mr. Wooley today?" I asked on approaching.

"Oh, it's you, Mrs. Hudson, is it?" he asked, squinting up into the sun at me as I thankfully set my grocery bags down at his feet. "Not too bad, all things considered. And you?"

"Weary," I admitted, "but well enough. Taking in a bit of sun, are you?"

"Doing it more for these old pins of mine than anything else," he replied, running bony hands along each leg. "You'll have to forgive me for not rising, though. By the time I managed to get myself up into a standing position, you'd be gone. Rheumatism," he added by way of explanation. "The sun seems to help. So whenever it decides to come out, so do I."

I offered up my sympathies with respect for his rheumatism while taking in the thin, sparse figure before me. A gray stubble of a beard encompassed a drawn face of a man perhaps no more than sixty who could have passed for seventy if it had not been for a pair of twinkling eyes that seemed to laugh at life itself. A nondescript bowler sat at a jaunty angle atop his head, and the ill-fitting coat and pants that hung over the skeletal frame along with the scuffed shoes completed the ensemble.

"Just my luck," he grinned, making light of his infirmity, "to end my days on this more often than not sunless little island of yours."

"Your accent," I smiled. "From Canada, are you?"

"The states," he answered.

"America? From what part?"

"Buffalo. Buffalo, New York, is where I was born. Left when I was thirteen and never been back since. Been everywhere else, though. Yep, ol' Peter Wooley has seen the elephant, he has."

"Seen the—elephant?"

"Seen it all, ma'am," he enlightened me. "And then some."

"You've been in the theater, have you?" I asked, remembering the aforementioned magic act.

"The theater!" he exclaimed with a chuckle. "That's a good one. No, nothing so grand as the theater. But, you're right in a way. Vaudeville, what you call music halls over here," he explained, "that was my bread and butter. Toured all over the states and up into Canada as well," he announced with no little pride.

"With your magic act?"

"Oh. I had lots of different acts at one time or another. Never did get top billing. Never was really all that good. If one act died I'd put together another one. More often than not at the management's request," he added with a knowing wink. "Why," he said, "I changed my act more often than I changed my shirt." (I believed him). "The Wooley Man— Soft Shoe and Funny Sayings, that was one of them. Mister Magic, The Professor and His Wonder Dog, they were all me," he laughed, displaying a row of rotted teeth in the process. "That dog act, though, that was the worst. Dang thing dropped dead of old age on me during a matinee performance in Scranton."

"Good heavens, whatever did you do?" I asked, completely caught up in it all.

"Picked up the dog, told the audience I had put him into a hypnotic trance, and tap-danced my way offstage."

"I don't believe a word of it," I laughed.

"It's as true as God made little green apples," he assured me. "It worked out okay in any event. Gave me an idea for my next act. I opened the following week in Altoona as Hypno the Hypnotist."

What an entertaining little fellow he was I thought; until a second glance at those long, spindly legs made me realize that while entertaining, he was certainly not little. No doubt if he'd been in a standing position he would be a man of Mr. Holmes's height at least.

So there he sat and there I stood while he continued to regale me with one humorous anecdote after another from his years onstage until, with curiosity getting the best of me, I asked how it was he ended up on our shores.

"The Shubert theatrical agency was putting a variety show together to tour England," I was informed. "Somehow or other my agent managed to get me booked on the show. 'Last on the bill but first in their hearts' that's Peter Wooley," he chuckled. "We spent three months playing London and touring the provinces. Did boffo business too, I might add. After the tour the troupe sailed back to New York but by that time I had decided to stay on here. Found me a pretty little gal in Liverpool, ol' Peter did," he added, in answer to my question. "We were hitched two weeks later. Millie, that was her name, said she always wanted to get into show biz so I came up with a routine for the two of us. Called it 'Wooley and the Missus.' Real cornpone, you understand, but the audience loved it. Best act I ever had. Then, just when everything was going good Millie took sick, sudden like, and died. That'd be ten years ago next month,'' he announced with the shoulders heaving in conjunction with a wistful sigh. ''What with me being so much older I always figured I'd be the first to go. But you never know, do you? After that, things were never quite the same. Found I didn't have the stamina or the interest any more for the footlights. 'Sides that, my health was never all that good. Nowadays I pick up the odd bit of pocket money on street corners with the magic act or as Mister Jolly the Clown at children's parties. Ha!'' he suddenly exclaimed, breaking out into a lopsided grin, ''bet'cha didn't think when you stopped by for a howdy-do you'd end up hearing an old man's life story, now did you?''

I agreed with a smile that I certainly didn't.

''Well, that's what happens when you stop to speak to strange men on the street,'' he added with a wink.

''Oh, Mr. Wooley,'' I laughed, ''you're incorrigible.''

''Incorrigible?'' The eyes peered up into mine. ''Is that good?''

''In your case,'' I answered good-humoredly, ''yes.'' I then mentioned that something he had spoken of earlier had interested me.

''And what would that be?'' he asked.

''Your hypnotist act,'' I answered. ''I speak of it because not only have I always found the subject fascinating but my friend, Mrs. Warner, and I were talking about it just the other day. It seems her dentist wanted to put her under as they say, to extract a tooth.''

''A dentist!'' he exclaimed, shaking his head in wonderment. ''Dentists are getting into the act too now, are they?'' He digested that little bit of information for a moment or two before asking what it was I wanted to know.

''Can you really put someone into a trance or is it just a trick of some sort?'' I asked.

''Oh, no. It's no trick,'' he assured me. ''If you know what you're doing. Some go under easier than others, some just partway and some you can't put under at all. Me, now,'' he went on, ''I was never what you'd call an expert at it so I'd always have a couple of ringers in the audience just in case.''

''Ringers?''

''Stooges, you might say,'' he answered. When I still looked a little puzzled, he elaborated. ''They'd be people I'd pay a dollar or two beforehand to come up on stage just in case I struck out. They'd be there to play along with anything I said.''

''Was there ever a time when you couldn't put someone under?''

''You know,'' he answered with a thoughtful scratch to that stubbled chin, ''I don't believe there was.''

''Then, why—?''

''Lack of confidence, I guess,'' was the sheepish reply. ''Then again, I was never all that keen on playing with people's minds. It's a tricky business, Mrs. Hudson.''

''Yes, I suppose you're right,'' I reluctantly agreed. ''But it can be entertaining. I remember, oh, this was back a number of years now, I saw an act where the hypnotist gave some people onstage a word to remember then later, when he repeated it, they'd start singing or scratching themselves and doing all sorts of silly things. I confess I had tears in my eyes from laughing so much.''

''Oh, sure,'' he nodded knowingly. ''I had the same routine in my act as well. It's what we call a posthypnotic suggestion. But, look here,'' he announced, ''if you want to know more about hypnosis, the fellah you oughta see is the Great Zambini. I'd say he's one of the best in the business. He'll be over at the Alhambra for another week. Top billing, too. Tell him ol' Peter Wooley sent you. Don't know if he'd remember me or not,'' he added, ''but it's worth a try.''

I thanked him for the suggestion but assured him he'd given me all the information I really needed. From what he told me it would appear Vi had made the right decision when it came to dentists and hypnotic trances. Perhaps sometime in the future when it was better understood by the medical profession, it would be a different matter. But, as for now, as Mr. Wooley had so succinctly put it, ''it's a tricky business.''

We exchanged a few more pleasantries until, realizing the lateness of the hour and the two gentlemen boarders I had at home waiting, none too patiently I would imagine, for their noonday meal, I retrieved my groceries and bid Mr. Peter Wooley a good morning with the promise of stopping by for another delightful chat when next we met.

It was mid-afternoon when I finally found time to sit myself down at the kitchen table for the purpose of reviewing the notes Vi had taken the previous evening at the Bramwell residence.

"Sounds like a right interesting bloke, that Mr. Wooley does," remarked my companion who, no doubt, had been going over in her mind the encounter I had related earlier to her between myself and our American neighbor down the street.

"What? Oh, yes, he is," I remarked off-handedly. "And from what he said you did well in not having a tooth out by hypnosis."

"Well, 'course I did," came the smug reply as she stood with her back to me at the counter preparing the two of us a nice fresh pot of tea. "Me women's inhibition told me that much."

"Intuition," I smiled, correcting her.

"Whatever," she shrugged, before asking if there was a biscuit or two left that we could have with our tea.

"There's some raisin buns I picked up this morning on the second shelf just to your left," I answered.

"Oh, lovely."

Thus, with the tea now brewed, the buns before us, and Vi's note pad at the ready, we set about the business of reviewing what had been said and perhaps, more importantly, what hadn't been said by those within the room on the night of the murder.

"Let's begin then, shall we?" I picked up her note pad, flipped open the first page, and let out a groan.

"What's all that about, eh?" was the indignant response from across the table.

"Your writing," I answered. "The first line reads, 'Mi Moon—gums—churudes.' Now, what on earth does that mean?"

" 'Ere, let's have a look. Why, Emma Hudson,"
she declared after no more than a brief glance, "it's
as plain as the nose on your face. It says, 'Mr.
Moore—games—charades.''

"Perhaps, dear," I replied, putting it as nicely as
I could, "it might be best if next time you confined
yourself to simply printing."

"Did the best I could, I did," she sulked.

"True enough," I agreed. "I only—oh, here's
something I didn't catch the first time around," I
said, interrupting myself as I scanned the first few
lines.

"What?"

"When playing charades, Mr. Moore says that
just before the murder they were trying to guess the
name of a book, if I read your writing correctly."

"Aye. So?"

"I may be wrong," I answered, "but I'm sure
Mrs. Bramwell said they were in the midst of trying
to find out the name of some famous composer."

"Well, what of it? Books, composers, what difference does it make, eh?"

"Probably none," I admitted. "But any little inconsistency is worth noting."

"Inconsistency," she repeated, making a face.
"Nit-picking, I calls it."

"Yes, well, first off," I stated, ignoring her
barbed remark, "we can at least set aside the question as to where each one was at the time the murder
was committed since, as you so once aptly put it,
they were all in the same ruddy room when it happened."

"Aye," she smiled, "that's right."

"Then the next logical step would be in deciding

who had the greater motive for wanting Edgar Bramwell dead.''

"Oh, well, that's easy enough, ain't it?"

"Is it? I wouldn't have thought so. Why do you say that?"

"Well, it'd be Mr. Moore, wouldn't it," she replied casually, picking up a raisin that had fallen from her bun onto the table, "what with losin' his job and all, I mean."

"Yes, I'd have to agree with you he does have motive. The politics of business have left him unemployed, plus an upcoming marriage hangs precariously in the balance. And no doubt in Arthur Moore's mind all because of the late and, it would seem in some quarters, unlamented Mr. Bramwell."

"Thing is though," questioned Vi, "if it was him, how'd he pull it off? Doesn't look all that clever to me."

"That's where you're wrong, m'girl," I corrected her. "Mr. Moore is nobody's fool. In fact," I added, "any one of them could have 'pulled it off' as you say."

"But, how'd you suppose it was done, eh?" she asked, munching away on the last remains of her bun.

"The question of how it was done would, I believe, best be left to another time. Right now I think we should focus on who it was that did it. And whoever it was," I continued on, "I still can't help but feel no matter how clever he or she was, an accomplice was needed. To shoot someone in a roomful of people with no one seeing it being done or hearing the shot, the murderer would have to have had someone else to help pull the strings from behind the curtain, so to speak.''

"So much for Mr. Moore, then,'' she chuckled.

"Why do you say that?''

"Well, I mean, can you imagine our spinster lady with the two names being his accomplice?''

"Miss Armstrong-Jones, you mean?''

"Aye. The one who thinks Mr. Bramwell shot himself.''

"But does she, really?'' I questioned. "It could have been a ruse on both their parts to head us off on another track.''

"Don't trust a one of 'em, do you, luv?'' she said, eyeing me thoughtfully.

"We can't afford to Vi,'' I stated. "Not if we want to see this through to a successful conclusion.''

"What about the MacPhails, then?'' she questioned. "Seem like a right nice couple, they do.''

"I couldn't agree with you more. But look at the situation young David MacPhail now finds himself in. Without the necessary funds to keep his plantation operational he'll lose everything. Motive enough, wouldn't you think?''

"Aye, right enough,'' she sighed in commiseration for the man. "But you'd think that Bramwell bloke would have put up the money for old times' sake, wouldn't you? I mean,'' she added, "what with them being old school chums and all.''

"Yes, but don't forget what Mr. Burke told us of Edgar Bramwell's amorous advances towards Patricia MacPhail and the fisticuffs that ensued between both men because of it.''

"But that were years ago,'' she countered.

"True. But for all we know Patricia may have

been the one love of Edgar Bramwell's life notwithstanding his marriage to Jane. In any event," I added, "it would appear that the murdered man had a long and unforgiving memory."

"And I always thought," added Vi, with a snicker of a smile, "the old saying was 'beware of a woman scorned.' "

"Obviously," I replied, returning the smile, "it works both ways." I put my cup to my lips, saw it was empty, and set it down.

"Want that filled up again, do you?" she asked on rising.

"Well, if you're getting up," I replied, "perhaps I will."

"Right. Might as well finish up the buns as well then. Otherwise," she added in all innocence, "they'll go stale, like."

"Stale? Why, I bought them only this morning."

"Aye, right enough. But," she added, fetching down the remaining two, "they don't last all that long, do they?"

"Not around here they don't," I smiled on returning to my notes and, as I did, I questioned myself as to whether Arthur Moore's loss of employment and marital status or lack of it would be enough reason for a man to commit murder. Then again, I reasoned, we all react differently to the various crises that confront us at one time or another along life's journey. Another man faced with the same situation might merely shake his fist toward the heavens and curse his misfortune, while another might find himself being eaten away inside by an all-consuming hatred that he believes can only be satisfied in seeking revenge by the very act of murder itself. Which of these men is Arthur Moore? And what of David MacPhail? Could not the same be said of him? Unfortunately, one cannot plumb the depths of another's soul during a few minutes' conversation. Though one wishes that she could. "And what of Roger Burke?"

"Eh?"

"Oh, I'm sorry, Vi. I hadn't realized I was speaking my thoughts aloud."

"You said," she queried, "what of Roger Burke? Well what about him?"

"You tell me," I said.

"Oh," she answered with a knowing wink, "quite the ladies' man he is, and no mistake."

I smiled. "You like him, don't you?"

"Yes I do," she replied defensively. "And why not, eh? Big strapping bloke like that. Sailing off to Africa like he does without so much as a by-your-leave to anyone. Having all sorts of adventures. Wish I were a man sometimes, I do. Don't you?"

"It would have its advantages," I admitted. "Being able to vote, to be paid a decent wage, and to come and go as one pleases are but a few of the privileges that spring immediately to mind. However, my dear Mrs. Warner," I added, "when you weigh that against the prospect of having to go off to war and coming back legless or armless, if you come back at all, it does—"

"'Ere," she exclaimed, stepping in with a most puzzled look on her face, "who's talking 'bout him going off to war, eh? Bound for Africa, he is, to search for a lost diamond mine."

"Oh, Vi," I sighed in a show of exasperation. "In the first place, I wasn't speaking of Mr. Burke specifically. And in the second place, if you check your

notes you'll see he isn't going off to Africa or anywhere else for that matter. Edgar Bramwell was shot
before financing for the expedition could be arranged
between the two men.''

After a perusal of her notes she grudgingly admitted I was right but brightened up when the
thought struck her with that being the case, Roger
Burke was the one man without motive. You don't
go putting a bullet into someone who's all set to
hand over a packet of money to you is how, I believe
she put it. And quite right she was, too.

Ah, but if it had been otherwise, we'd have a man,
Roger Burke, who, after hacking his way through
the jungle to get a half-mad with fever Edgar Bramwell back to the coast and onto a ship for England,
being refused financing by the very man whose life
he had, for all intents and purposes, saved. However,
such was not the case. And, in any event, it helped
whittle down the list of suspects.

"You've not eaten your bun, luv," spoke Vi, eyeing the uneaten treat before me. "Not going to let it
just sit there, are you?"

As to whether I was or wasn't, a sudden ringing
of the front doorbell set aside for the moment any
answer I might have given.

"Now, who on earth could that be, I wonder?" I
said on rising from the table.

"If it's someone for Mr. Holmes or Doctor Watson," sang out Vi as I made my way down the hall,
"tell 'em they won't be back till late, like."

It was apparent on opening the door that the caller
was not seeking out either one of our illustrious
boarders unless Mr. Holmes's latest client was a lad
of no more than twelve.

"Missus Hudson?" he asked, thrusting out a small white envelope before me.

"The very same." I smiled on accepting it.

"I'm to wait for an answer," he said on my withdrawing the note and scanning its contents.

Mrs. Bramwell, it seemed, was not one to waste any time, for she had requested I meet with her at seven o'clock that very night. While it would, I thought, afford me the opportunity of speaking with her household staff as well, in all honesty I would rather have put it off until the morrow, having put in a rather long day. However, I had long since realized from Mr. Holmes's erratic schedules as well as from my own that as consulting detectives we did not always have the luxury of setting our own hours. Thus, with a resigned sigh, I informed the lad I would meet with the lady at the designated time.

He received the information with a nod of understanding but remained rooted to the spot while continuing to stare up at me with questioning eyes.

"Oh," I said, "yes, of course. Something for your trouble, right?"

A smile of anticipation emerged on that elfin face which just as quickly disappeared when I offered up my apologies for not having a bit of change handy. "Tell you what," I said, "how'd you like a nice fresh raisin bun, eh?"

The smile reappeared.

"Right, then. You get yourself down to the kitchen and tell the lady there that Mrs. Hudson says it's all right."

"Oh, thank-ee, mum," he beamed, taking off down the hallway.

That is, I thought, if she hasn't already eaten it.

FOUR

Back to Mayfair

⟡ HAVING RETURNED AS requested to the Bramwell residence, I found myself once again in the study with the lady of the house seated, as before, behind the desk, and I, as before, to the front of it. As for Violet, she had remained at home. As I believed my stay would not be of a lengthy duration, I felt there was little need for the both of us to put in an appearance. Surprisingly, my companion accepted my decision amicably enough by stating she could put her time to good use by catching up on her ironing.

"What you tell me, Mrs. Hudson, is most disturbing," spoke Jane Bramwell, after I had related to her what had transpired with those I had questioned on the previous evening. "To present me," she said, "with motives for murder, motives held by friends of both my late husband and myself, leaves

78

me at a loss for words.'' She picked up a quill pen and, in a pensive mood, toyed aimlessly with the feathers.

I waited a moment or two before stating that although we now have before us personal reasons for revenge by at least two of the men who were present within the room, it would be presumptuous of me to point a finger of suspicion at any one person at this point in time. I added that whether or not Miss Armstrong-Jones or Mrs. MacPhail was a party to either man's actions was also, at least for the present, mere conjecture.

While I was of the opinion that the murder could not have been committed by some unknown intruder, such was my concern for her, misguided though it may have been, that I sought to soften the harsh reality of my findings.

''There's no need to cushion me from the truth, Mrs. Hudson,'' she said, raising her eyes level to mine.

Good heavens, I thought, it was as if she had read my mind. And although her words, as I say, gave me a bit of a start, I made no reply but awaited her continuance.

''I spoke to you,'' she confided, ''of what you had told me as being most disturbing and, in truth, it is. But I would be less than honest with you, dear lady, if I did not confess I have long suspected in my heart of hearts that it had to be someone in the room that night who fired the fatal shot. Or perhaps they all had a hand in it in some fashion or another,'' she said, tossing the pen aside. ''One doesn't want to think such things, mind you, but I must be realistic, mustn't I? I can't tell you how relieved I'll be,'' she

added, exhaling a weary sigh, "when this whole
thing is finaly cleared up."

"And if it's not?"

"And if it's not?" she repeated. "Why, whatever
do you mean?"

"It could very well end up as an unsolved murder
on the police files," I answered, "if efforts by all
parties concerned are of no avail in finding the murderer."

She stared at me for the longest moment before
asking, "Do you really believe such a thing could
happen?"

"I can only state," I answered with a smile of
reassurance, "that I will do my best to see that it
doesn't. Now tell me," I asked, "how did everyone
fare with the inspector last night?"

"It was not the most pleasant of evenings," she
confessed. "I'm afraid our nerves are strung out like
piano wires. Questions, questions, questions, and
none of us with answers to the inspector's liking.
For a moment or two I thought both he and Roger
would come to blows. Fortunately," she added with
a little laugh, "it all ended peacefully enough."

"What's this? Mr. Burke?" I exclaimed. "I
would never have thought it of him. Seems like quite
a good-natured chap, really."

"Yes, but you must understand," she stressed,
"the poor man has been under a great deal of strain
of late. More so than the others, I should think."

"You refer to his lost diamond mine, I take it.
Yes," I went on without waiting for a reply, "when
one thinks of him and your late husband forging a
partnership that could have resulted in untold wealth
should the existence of the mine be proved and then,

to see that dream snatched away from him by Mr. Bramwell's untimely death, it must have been quite devastating to say the least. A lost diamond mine, indeed," I added, "in every sense of the word."

"I'm afraid I don't quite follow you," said she, eyeing me most curiously. "There were no plans for a partnership between Edgar and Mr. Burke. It would appear you've been misinformed, Mrs. Hudson."

I confess I was completely taken aback by her pronouncement and could only splutter that I had been under the impression her husband had agreed on backing the expedition financially.

"Oh, at one time he did, yes," she replied. "But after Edgar had sought out the society's president, Mr. Muir, for his advice and found it was that gentleman's considered opinion that mounting such an expedition would be sheer folly, my husband decided against the venture."

"And Roger Burke," I asked, "he knew of this?"

"Yes, of course," she replied. "He told you otherwise, did he?"

I passed on her question by asking another. "Why then did he attend the party? Surely the relationship between the two men could not have been all that cordial."

"Evidently," she answered, "the invitation was sent prior to my husband's decision. Mr. Burke came, no doubt, to see if he might change Edgar's mind. But that of course," she added, "would be mere speculation on my part."

I nodded thoughtfully while mentally digesting the information that had been placed before me. So, Roger Burke had lied. But why? The obvious answer was that he was guilty and had sought to cover up his motive for murder. Then again, it could very well be that, being innocent, he had no wish to be singled out as a suspect, prime or otherwise, by revealing that a business arrangement with the murdered man had turned sour. In any case, his name would now have to be added to my list. Putting that thought aside for the moment, I turned my attention back to the lady to inquire of her how she would describe the relationship that had existed between her and her late husband.

"Now, that," she replied in a mockingly reproachful manner, "sounds very much like one of the inspector's questions. Fortunately," she smiled, "it is one that I can answer. I don't believe," she said, "Edgar ever regretted marrying me. As for myself, I certainly never wanted for anything as you can see." She followed that statement with an airy wave of the hand as if to encompass the house and all its worldly possessions. "Then of course," she added, "our marriage was blessed by the most loving daughter that ever a mother could have wished for."

"Yes," I agreed, "she is a dear little thing. But, as for yourself and your husband, you got on well, did you?"

"I should like to think so," she answered simply.

"Then there was never any—" I was cut short by a tapping at the door simultaneous with its opening. Turning halfway round in my chair, I saw Mrs. Birdie poke her head in and, on taking note of me, apologized to her mistress for her intrusion.

Jane Bramwell graciously brushed the apology aside and beckoned her in, questioning the child's governess as to whether there was any problem.

"Oh, no, none at all, Mrs. Bramwell," the woman hastily assured her. "The thing of it is, I've just put Dorothy to bed and she's waiting for you to come up and say goodnight."

"In that case," responded the lady of the house with a mother's smile, "I'll be right up. Thank you, Nanny." Then, turning to me, "Was there anything else, Mrs. Hudson?"

"No," I answered, "at least not for the present. Although," I added, as we rose in tandem from our chairs, "I would like to have a little chat, if I may, with Mrs. Birdie as well as your staff, if that's convenient."

"I don't see why it wouldn't be," she answered on crossing the floor. "You may speak in here if you wish, after which I'm sure Mrs. Birdie wouldn't mind introducing you to the others." She paused at the door. "I'll see you before you leave, then?"

On my assuring her that she would, she turned to exit the room but was halted by my calling out after her. "Mrs. Bramwell, your pendant," I said, on spotting and retrieving the object from its precarious position on the edge of the desk. "I'm afraid it's come off on you again."

"Oh, my stars, you're right," she cried, clasping a hand to her throat. "I simply must have Martin see what he can do about fixing it. It was a gift from my husband, you know," she added as I handed it to her. "Thank you ever so much, Mrs. Hudson. Till later, then."

Well, at least I've been of some help, I thought. Lord knows I haven't been able to offer up much else as yet in the way of a solution to the crime.

Still, I told myself, in the hope of reviving my flagging spirits, the case is young and I've yet to question the staff and Mrs. Birdie.

The child's governess and I exchanged hesitant smiles, followed in turn by an awkward silence that ended when I inquired whether she was aware of the reason for my being there.

"Yes," she answered, "I had heard from Mrs. Bramwell. I was ever so pleased she confided in me. Such is my station that she wouldn't as a rule. Nor would I have known," she added, "if it had been left up to the servants."

"Oh, and why is that?"

"Within the social structure of a household such as this," she informed me, "a governess is not taken into the confidence of the family nor do the servants consider her one of them. We are, for all intents and purposes," she added quite good-naturedly, "neither fish nor fowl. It's true then, is it?"

The question was so completely out of context I was obliged to answer with one of my own. "True? What is?"

"That you and your lady friend are detectives."

It was true enough, I informed her, adding that I had a question or two for her as well. I began by stating that from what Scotland Yard had been able to establish the murder had occurred sometime between the hours of ten and eleven o'clock. Could she, I asked, tell me what she was doing and where she was within that time period?

"In the child's bedroom fast asleep," she answered without a moment's hesitation. "As I have already told the inspector, I had put Dorothy to bed earlier that evening and, after reading her a story, I had set the book aside and continued rocking in the chair while waiting for her to drift off. I'm afraid,'' she confessed with a smile, ''I must have dozed off myself as well, for when Martin came looking for me to tell me what had happened, he found me fast asleep in the rocker.''

''And when he woke you?''

''Out the room and down the stairs I went double-quick with Martin following close behind,'' she answered. ''When we got downstairs the men were all milling about outside the door. It was closed by that time so I never did get in to see poor Mr. Bramwell. Which was just as well in any case, from what they tell me. I mean, you know, 'bout how he looked and all,'' she added with a slight involuntary shudder.

''And as to Mrs. Bramwell,'' I asked, ''she was—?''

''In the study here, with the other ladies. 'Course I went right in and tried to comfort her as best I could, what with the dear thing being quite beside herself with grief, as well you can imagine.''

Although her movements as she had related them to me fell in line with what the others had told me regarding those moments after the shooting had occurred, there was one thing she hadn't mentioned that struck me as odd. Or was I merely grasping at straws? Maybe. In any event it was something that merited deeper thought at a later date. Right now, there were one or two other questions I had in mind. ''Mrs. Birdie,'' I asked, ''how would you describe the relationship that existed between Mrs. Bramwell and her husband?''

The question proved to be somewhat disconcerting for the woman, for I noted that the affable Mrs.

Birdie immediately tensed up on the asking of it.
"Their relationship?" she repeated. "I don't—I
mean, that's not for the likes of me to say, is it? No,
Mrs. Hudson," she stated quite firmly on sensing a
rebuttal on my part, "Mavis Birdie is not one to be
telling tales out of school, so to speak. Not that
there's tales to be told, mind," she added defensively.

"I can assure you," I answered with a smile in
the wish of setting her her mind at ease, "you'll be
telling no tales out of school. Mrs. Bramwell has
already indicated to me the marriage was not a
happy one. I only seek confirmation from you."

Which was true, up to a point. The key word being "indicated." For Jane Bramwell, in her attempt
to neatly sidestep my questions, had unwittingly answered them. She believed, she had said, that her
husband had never regretted marrying her. A strange
reply, at best, I thought, when a simple "my husband and I loved each other very much" would have
sufficed. Indeed, never, I had noted, was the word
love used in connection with the marriage, except
when speaking of her child. And then it was ". . . a
most loving daughter that ever a mother could wish
for." Not, one would have thought ". . . a most loving daughter that both my husband and I could ever
have wished for." When I had asked point-blank
whether they had got on well together she had answered that she liked to think so. That, in itself, told
me nothing, and she knew it. It was all very sad,
really. For how can one describe a happy marriage
without mentioning love? Unless—Mrs. Bramwell
had tried and failed.

"And you want me to confirm what my mistress

said about it being a loveless marriage, do you?'' questioned Mrs. Birdie, now seemingly more at ease with herself and with me. "I can do that right enough what with his drinking and all. She told you that, did she—about his drinking, I mean?''

"We touched on a number of points," I answered, while thinking how ironic it was that I was now playing Jane Bramwell's game of tiptoeing through the woman's questions. "Drinking could very well have been one of them," I added innocently enough.

"I should think that it would be!" she huffed. "Oh, I know what they say 'bout speaking ill of the dead, but I'll tell you straight out, Mrs. Hudson, he was a holy terror when he'd been in his cups, and no two ways about it. Why, many's the night there'd be a battle royal loud enough to wake the child and set her to wailing. Not that he'd mind. Didn't care tuppence for her. Always berating Mrs. Bramwell, he was, for not being able to give him a son. Lovely woman that she is, as if she could do anything about it.''

Visibly upset by her outpouring, she removed her glasses to dab a pudgy finger across her moistened eyes.

"And during those nights of drunkenness and verbal abuse he was not above beating her, was he,'' I said, putting the question in the form of a statement in remembrance of the bruised arm Jane Bramwell had tried to hide when first we met. Indeed, for traces of discoloration to have remained for so many days after the original injury, one could only speculate with dismay the extent of force that would had to have been applied.

As to the question of beatings, Mavis Birdie, in

between a sniffle or two, announced she would say no more one way or the other. In truth, there was no need. I had my answer. And, while grateful to her for what I had learned, the frustrating thing about it all was that I now found myself with yet another name on which the shadow of suspicion fell—the very woman who had hired me! Although a wife bullied and beaten by her husband was certainly motive enough, I found it all rather unsettling. I had hoped to whittle down the list, not add to it. Nevertheless, I thanked Mrs. Birdie for her time and cooperation and, on her opening of the door to take our leave, we came face to face with a very surprised and startled butler.

"Oh," he said on regaining his composure, "I was just coming in to see if there was anything you require, Mrs. Hudson."

Was he really? I wonder. It appeared to me, as it must have to Mrs. Birdie, that the young man had been standing just outside the door for who knows how long? If true, it could be at best no more than mere curiosity. Lord knows butlers have been eavesdropping outside doors ever since there've been butlers. "The only thing I require," I answered with a smile, "is your time."

"My time?"

"Mrs. Hudson would like a word or two with you, Martin," spoke the governess.

"Oh, I see. Yes, of course. Here in the study then?"

"That'd be fine," I answered.

"I'll be leaving you then, Mrs. Hudson," announced the woman as I turned to follow Martin back into the room.

"Yes, thank you, Mrs. Birdie," I acknowledged over my shoulder. "Perhaps we'll talk again."

As to my question and answer session with the Bramwell butler it proceeded along amicably enough although I did at first find his responses to be somewhat guarded. This I put down to human nature. For we all, I find, tend to tense up when put on the defensive by having to justify our words and/or actions to a second party.

Eventually he relaxed, and while that in itself boded well, I learned little I could construe as being significant. Yes, he had entered the room on one or two occasions on the night of the murder to see to their needs and no, he hadn't noticed anything out of the ordinary. They were, he informed me, busily engaged in enjoying themselves in a game of charades. As to his whereabouts at the time of the murder he had, he said, gone down to the wine cellar at Mr. Bramwell's request to replenish the party's dwindling supply. On returning he came upon Mr. MacPhail rushing out the room to inform him as to what had just occurred. At that gentleman's urgent request he immediately left to inform the police. "But not before," he stated, "checking to see whether Mrs. Birdie, Mrs. Smollett, and Rose were safe from harm. You understand," he added, "we were all in quite a turmoil and the thought that some madman or other might be loose somewhere in the house—well, need I say more?"

"And you found the cook and the maid—?"

"Fast asleep in their rooms."

"And Mrs. Birdie?"

"She was asleep as well," he answered. "In the child's bedroom."

"I see," I replied thoughtfully, masking my disappointment. Not, I might add, in his reaffirming the governess's story, but from what I had learned from all concerned. Each one in his or her own way confirmed the other's account of the events that had taken place. How I wished there had been some glaring discrepancy I could have pounced on. And then the butler inadvertently provided it when I asked his opinion as to the state of the Bramwell marriage.

"I would say it was one of devotion," he stated simply.

His answer caught me completely off-guard though I did my best not to show it. "Devotion?" I repeated, seeking an elaboration on his part.

"Yes," he answered matter-of-factly, "it would be my opinion that the two of them were devoted to each other."

"But," I pressed, "I had heard that Mr. Bramwell drank to excess on many an occasion."

"What man doesn't?" was the rhetorical response. "I don't mind telling you, Mrs. Hudson," he added as that boyishly handsome face broke into a grin, "I've been known to have gone a bit overboard myself on many an occasion."

"But did not his drinking cause, shall we say, a bit of a problem between him and his wife?" I asked, alluding indirectly to what the governess had told me.

"A problem?" he mused. "No more, I'd say, then it would in any marriage."

"Then, to sum up, you'd say they were more or less—?"

"Devoted."

There was that word again. Though not one it

would be safe to assume Mrs. Birdie would have used. Which one of the two was lying?

Odd as it may seem perhaps neither of them were. From the butler's point of view, that is to say, the male perspective, it would have been a marriage not unlike many another. A loving husband one day, in a drunken stupor the next, physically abuses his wife who, should she seek to file a complaint, knows only too well she would find little redress of her grievances in court. The idea of a man's home being his castle and those who dwell within his subjects still remains, even as I write, an unwritten law firmly entrenched within the pysche of the English male. Perhaps Martin had been brought up in just such a family environment. As such, their marriage would have appeared to him to have been the norm. On the distaff side, Mrs. Birdie would, of course, have been appalled at Edgar Bramwell's behavior. And rightly so.

These thoughts I carried with me as Martin, with my inquiry at an end, escorted me out of the room and down to the kitchen where after a proper round of introductions he left me with Mrs. Smollett, the cook. She was a tiny woman with a large mass of gray hair tied up in a bun in back. She was sitting at the end of a great wooden slab of a table enjoying a cup of tea with the maid, Rose. And quite a pretty young thing Rose was, too. And while I did enjoy the cup of tea I was offered, other than Rose revealing her unrequited feelings for Martin, I learned nothing of any importance regarding the crime from either one of them.

"Oh, you should see him, you should, Mrs. Hudson," gushed Rose, "when he's sittin' up there behind the wheel of that lovely automobile in his cap and goggles, wearin' his yellow duster, white gloves and all. Looks ever so dashing, he does. Promised to give me a spin round the block, he did.''

'' 'Ere, now, m'girl,'' snapped the elder of the two women, ''don't you go telling Mrs. Hudson any of your lies.''

''Well,'' pouted the girl, trying to put the best possible light on it, ''he would have if I'd of asked him.''

''I'm sure he would have,'' I answered in a smile.

''Not our Martin,'' vouched the cook most vehemently. ''Keeps to himself, he does. And quite right, too. He's got no time for the likes of you, Rose Tuttle.''

Not wishing to become embroiled in a maid's romantic entanglements, imaginary or otherwise, I thanked them both for the tea and their time and found my way back to the front hallway, where I met the lady of the house descending the staircase.

''Ah, there you are, Mrs. Hudson,'' she said, continuing her way downward. ''You've met and spoken to everyone you wished to, have you?''

''Yes, thank you, Mrs. Bramwell, I have.''

She nodded and paused on the last step. ''And you learned—?''

''Only that they know as little of what happened that night as do you,'' I answered. ''Nevertheless,'' I continued on in a somewhat more hopeful vein, ''I'm of the opinion the mystery of it all will unravel itself sooner or later.'' It was an ambiguous comment at best but one I hoped for now would suffice. Evidently it did, for she stepped forward, placing her hands in mine, and assured me that if anyone could get to the bottom of it it would be yours truly.

"And now, my dear Mrs. Hudson," she added with her hands still pressed in mine, "I wonder if I might ask a favor of you?"

After such praiseworthy comment I was only too human to oblige.

"Certainly, Mrs. Bramwell, ask away."

"I wonder if you'd mind awfully popping up to say goodnight to Dorothy? I told her you were here and, well, it seems she took quite a fancy to you the other day. Though I should add I did make mention of you being a lady detective which seemed to have made quite an impression on her."

Of course I readily accepted and, after being given directions to the child's room, I ascended the stairs, found the door, and entered.

A small lamp aglow on a bedside table afforded me a glimpse of the child half-hidden beneath the covers of a canopied bed.

"Oh, it's you, Mrs. Hudson!" she exclaimed on my calling out her name. "I knew you'd come."

"Yes, but mind, I can't stay too long," I answered as she set about propping up the pillow in back of her.

"Mommy says you're a detective. That's something like a policeman, isn't it?"

"Yes," I answered with a smile. "Something like a policeman."

"Do you put bad people in jail?"

"I sometimes see to it that's where they end up."

"Will you find the murderous scoundrel that killed my daddy? That's what Nanny calls him, a murderous scoundrel. What's a scoundrel?"

"Not a very nice man," I answered. "And, yes,

I hope to catch him very soon if I can."

"You can sit in Nanny's chair if you like," she said, indicating a padded rocker placed alongside the bed.

"Just for a minute or two then," I answered and, on easing myself down into it, added, "You must have loved your father very much."

"Yes, I suppose I did," she answered after a moment or two of thought. "I just wish I had known him ever so much better, then I'm sure he would have liked me."

I felt my heart break. What a terribly sad thing to hear. If William and I had been blessed with just such a child—How ironic, I thought, that I was put into the position of finding the murderer of such a man as Edgar Bramwell. I don't think I would have liked him very much. No, I don't think I would have liked him very much at all. "You mustn't talk like that, Dorothy," I said on turning my attention back to the child. "I'm sure your father in his own way loved you very much." A lie. But what else could I have said?

"I should like to think so," she answered a little wistfully before asking, quite unexpectedly, if I would read her a story.

"A story!" I exclaimed. "Goodness gracious, whatever would your mother say, or Nanny too, for that matter. It's time you went to sleep, little lady. Mustn't keep the sandman waiting, you know."

"Oh, please, Mrs. Hudson," pleaded that angelic face. "It won't take long. It's just a little story. Mommy or Nanny reads it to me every night."

"What, the same story?" I chuckled.

"It's my favorite one in the whole world," she

announced, as if that in itself justified the rereading of it. "Please?"

How could I refuse? "Where is it then?"

"There," she said, breaking out into a smile, "on the table."

I leaned over and picked it up. "Why, I know this one from *my* childhood," I said with a smile of remembrance for days long past. "Isn't this the one about a miller's daughter having to spin gold out of straw for the king?"

"Yes, yes!" she exclaimed. "And she couldn't do it. Then one night a little man crept in and said he would do it for her if she could tell him his name."

"Knowing full well," I added, becoming quite caught up in it all, "that no one in the world would ever guess it. But wasn't he overheard singing a little tune about himself and wasn't that how—?"

"The girl found out his name," interjected Dorothy, as those little eyes fairly danced with excitement.

"Which was—?"

"Rumpelstiltskin!" we chorused together followed by a peal of laughter.

And so it was that a "lady detective" in search of a murderer ended her evening beside a bed reading a fairy story to a little girl.

FIVE

One Step Forward

⟡ WHILE I ADMIT the information I had accumulated would no doubt prove helpful to the investigation in the long run, I was more than grateful to at last be home and was eagerly looking forward to a good night's rest. There'd be time enough to sort out the who, what, where, and why of it tomorrow, I told myself, as I gently eased open the bedroom door in the expectation of finding Violet fast asleep. To my surprise I found her wide awake, sitting up in bed reading.

"Decided to come home after all, did you?" was the snide little comment I received as her eyes narrowed in on me over the pages of her book.

"Sorry, Vi, I was longer than I thought I'd be," I answered with a yawn as I sank down on my side of the bed to unbutton my shoes. "What's that you're reading?"

"One of Doctor Watson's stories about him and Mr. Holmes solvin' some crime or other. I remember reading about it in the papers some time back but I can't remember who the murderer was."

"You could always go upstairs and ask them," I replied with a smile. "By the way, have you seen my nightgown? The pink flannel one?"

"It's folded up nice like, under your pillow. What, go upstairs now? Oh, they'd like that, I'm sure. 'Course,'' she added with a wink, "I could always turn to the last page. Find out soon enough then."

"Would that we could do the same," I answered, kicking my shoes aside and slipping out of my dress.

"How'd you mean?"

"Just think how nice it would be if we could turn to the last 'page' of our investigation to find out not only who it was that murdered Edgar Bramwell but also how the deed was done. Unfortunately," I added, removing the flannel nightgown from 'neath the pillow, "I'm afraid we still have quite a few 'pages' to go."

"Aye," my companion remarked dryly, "and so far all of them blank."

Having at last made myself ready for bed (a tiresome ritual exceeded only in the amount of time required of it by the reversal of the entire procedure in the morning) I quickly snuggled myself down under the covers with a body that sought a good night's rest but with a mind that was not of the same accord. Snatches of conversation heard earlier that evening whirled round my brain along with the unanswered questions that they raised.

"Well?" questioned Vi, snapping her book shut and laying it alongside the table lamp.

"Well, what?" I mumbled.

"Well, what, she says! 'Ere, what you think I've been waiting up to hear? What happened at the Bramwell's, eh?"

Although I would have dearly loved to have drifted off, heavy as my body felt, tired as my eyes were, it would, I thought, set my mind to rest if I unburdened myself with an accounting of all I had seen and heard. I propped myself up on one elbow and related to Vi as best I could the gist of the conversations I had had with Mrs. Bramwell and the household staff adding, as well, the little bedtime story episode with Dorothy. On hearing the reasons for my including not only Roger Burke on our list but the name of Jane Bramwell as well, Violet, as can be imagined, was left completely flabbergasted.

"Fancy a nice man like Roger Burke telling lies nice as you please 'bout how young Bramwell was going to put up the money for that so-called lost diamond mine of his. It just goes to show you, Em, you can't trust a murder suspect any farther than you can throw your shadow. And," she huffed, "as for Jane Bramwell, I'd of put a bullet in that husband of hers myself, I would, if I'd of known what he'd been up to. Why, in all our married years my Bert never so much as raised a hand to me."

"Nor William to me," I added.

"God bless 'em," she sighed. "But, 'ere, Em, I mean, suspecting Mrs. Bramwell herself—why, she's the lady we're working for!"

"True," I agreed. "But if we are to follow the proper procedures then technically, since motive is there, I thought it only right that her name be included as well."

"If this keeps up," remarked my companion, "we'll have half of London on our list, we will."

Although Violet intended her remark as a humorous aside, we both knew that an ever-growing list of suspects wouldn't make our investigation any easier. As for myself, I had hoped we'd now be at a stage where we could concentrate on one particular individual. Obviously, it hadn't quite turned out that way. "Perhaps Vi, it's time, as William would have said," I announced, referring to my late seafaring husband's penchant for a nautical turn of phrase, "to drop anchor and chart ourselves a new course. In other words," I continued on, "it might be best if we focused our attention not on who did it but on how it was done. But that," I added, hoping she'd take the hint as I returned head to pillow, "is something we can talk about tomorrow." Then, to make doubly sure—"Turn the light out if you're finished reading, would you, dear? There's a luv."

"Right you are then," she answered. "Unless," she added impishly, "you'd like me to read you a fairy tale or two 'fore you drifts off."

The following afternoon found me seated before the fireplace in the parlor busily engaged in sorting through a collection of old clothing.

"Thought we were giving that lot away to the church," spoke Violet on entering the room and taking a seat opposite.

"We are," I answered. "But I noticed there are a few blouses and skirts with a button or two missing. And," I added, reaching into my wicker sewing basket to extract the appropriate needle and thread, "I wouldn't dream of handing them over in the condition they're in."

"Really, Em," remarked my companion in a show of disdain, "as if the poor beggars what gets 'em could care one way or t'other."

"Oh, Vi."

" 'Ere," she said, eyeing two particular items of apparel, "isn't that Doctor Watson's old smoking jacket and one of Mr. Holmes's suits you have there?"

"It is indeed," I smiled. "Both gentlemen, I'm happy to say, were kind enough to donate them to the cause."

" 'Bout time they got rid of them, if you ask me. Why," she said, on reaching over to pick up Mr. Holmes's trousers, "the backside's worn so shiny you could use it for a mirror, you could."

"As if the poor begger that gets it could care one way or the other," I quipped.

"Got me there, Em," she laughed.

As I continued on with my sewing, Violet, aside from her initial outburst, remained unusually quiet and, I might add, somewhat fidgety. "Well go on," I said, "say it."

" 'Ere," she questioned, "how'd you know I was wanting to say anything?"

"I've known you long enough to know all the signs," I answered.

"Like as not you know what I'm going to say then," she shot back.

"No, but no doubt you'll tell me."

Silence. Then, "The thing is," she said at last, "I were just wondering if you've spoke to Mr. Holmes about this here Bramwell business."

"He knows that we're working on it, if that's what you mean," I answered.

"Well," she hedged, "it's not that so much. I mean—"

"You mean," I said, rummaging around in my sewing basket for a button similar to one missing from the good doctor's jacket, "have I approached Mr. Holmes with regard to any help he might be able to offer us. The answer," I added before she had time to reply, "is no."

"You're a stubborn one you are, Emma Hudson, and no mistake."

In manner calm and collected I informed my companion that stubbornness played no part in it, adding that if we were to seek out Mr. Holmes for assistance every time we came up against a blank wall, so to speak, then what was the point in taking on this or any other case?

"I suppose you're right," she sighed. "I just wish we had some answers of our own."

"Aha!" I sang out. "I've got it."

"What! You mean you know how it was done?"

"What? Oh, no, no," I admitted somewhat shamefacedly. "I mean I found a button for Doctor Watson's jacket."

"You found a—" Violet rolled her eyes heavenward in a show of exasperated annoyance. "Leastways one of us has her mind on the case," she sniped. "And I don't need to be saying which one."

"I assure you," I said trying to make the best of it, "notwithstanding a missing button or two, I think of nothing else."

"Well, I don't know about you," she replied, "but I've got what you might call a theory or two on how the murder was committed, I have."

"You have?" Quite taken aback by this latest revelation, I laid my sewing aside and gave her my complete attention.

"Now, just suppose," she began, "that the night before the shooting the murderer sneaks into the house and drills a hole in the wall from the hallway into the room itself. Then the next night when they all gets together drinking and carrying on like, he sneaks back in, puts his rifle into the hole, pulls the trigger, and quicker than you can say Bob's your uncle, young Bramwell's as dead as a dormouse."

I admit that for a moment or two there was a stunned silence on my part. "And that's it?" I said at last.

"Aye," beamed Violet, seemingly quite pleased with herself. "What do you think, eh?"

"Well," I answered after some hesitation, "there are one or two things that don't quite fit with what we already know. You see, dear," I said, as pleasantly as possible in order not to ruffle a feather or two, "in the first place there would have to be two holes drilled. One for the weapon, the second for the murderer to see through. But in any case, if there were any holes drilled into the wall they would have been noticed by now. And in the second place the murder weapon was a handgun not a rifle. And in the third place you've no explanation for the shot not being heard. But never mind, luv, at least you came up with an idea to the mystery of it, which is more than I can say for myself."

"Aye, well like I say," was the dejected response, "it were just one of my theories."

"You've another?"

"Aye," she replied. "They were all drugged."

"Drugged?"

"That's right. The murderer puts summat funny in everybody's drink. Then when they all collapse in a heap on the floor he pulls out his gun and shoots Mr. Bramwell. Then when they all wakes up who's the wiser for it, eh? That's why know one knows what happened. They were all drugged, see?"

Oh, dear, this was almost as bad as her first idea. But rather than dismiss it out of hand I pretended to give it some thought by asking whatever gave her the idea that they could have been drugged.

"It came to me the other night in bed," she answered, perking up by my show of interest. "I was half asleep when I thought I heard a noise outside. But I couldn't be sure like, if I had or not. You know how it is when you're neither one nor the other. Awake or asleep, I mean."

I nodded that I did.

"It were then that it came to me what Mrs. MacPhail had said on the night we were questioning her."

"Oh, and what was that?"

"That she thought she had heard a shot that sounded like it were a long way off but she couldn't be sure. Just like the noise I thought I had heard laying there in me bed all drowsy like."

"Yes, go, on."

"Well, I knew she couldn't have been standing there in the middle of the ruddy floor fast asleep so I figures that she and the rest of 'em must have been—"

"Drugged. Yes, I see. With the drug, for whatever reason, not having quite the same effect on her as the others, she would have been vaguely aware of a shot being fired."

"Aye, that's right."

"Yes, well, the thing of it is, dear," said I, putting it as diplomatically as I could, "not only would they have to have had, to use your own words, 'collapsed in a heap on the floor' at the same time but, each one, with the exception of the murderer himself, would have had to reawaken at the same moment. Otherwise the one who awakened first would be aware that they had been drugged. In any event, it's hard to imagine them all springing back up into consciousness without being aware of what had taken place."

Violet's face sagged in disappointment.

"Never mind, old girl," I added with a comforting smile, "it wasn't all that bad an idea." A white lie. But where's the harm? "At least," I admitted, "you were able to come up with an idea or two which, as I say, is more than I can lay claim to. Oh, by the way," I added, on returning my attention back to the good doctor's jacket, "as soon as I've got this button sewed on, these clothes will be ready to be dropped off at the church whenever one of us finds the time to—" I stopped in mid-sentence as an idea suddenly popped into my head. As I began to mull it over, Vi spoke up.

" 'Ere," she said, "what's the matter with you, eh?"

"What? Oh, an idea—I just had an idea," I mumbled, still deeply engrossed in thought.

"Must be a right good one then to screw up your face summat like that."

"Maybe. Maybe not."

"Let's hear it then."

"The thing is," I said slowly, "you could be right."

"I could? 'Bout what?"

"It's just possible that they *were* drugged."

"What!" she exclaimed. "After all you've been sayin' about how—"

"No, no, Vi," I interrupted. "You misunderstand me. I'm not speaking of pellets of powder being dropped into a glass."

"How, then?"

I hesitated for a moment or two before at last giving voice to my idea. "By hypnosis," I stated. With that, Violet gave me the oddest look, which, if truth be told, was no more than I had expected from her.

"Having me on, are you, Em?" she asked with a half-smile on that now puzzled face.

"I assure you I'm not," I answered haughtily. "You asked me and I told you. I'm simply stating," I went on by way of explanation, "it may have been that instead of some alien substance being added to their drink the possibility is there that it was done simply by the power of suggestion."

"By this here hypnosis business? Is that what you mean?"

"Yes."

"Well, I suppose it's no better nor worse an idea than that of sticking a rifle through a hole in the wall if it comes to that," she said, evidently resigning herself to the idea. "Get on with it then."

"Get on with it?"

"Aye. How were it done? Who hypnotized who?"

"Yes, well," I hedged, "I don't have all the answers as yet. But just suppose," I went on, warming

up to the idea, "the murderer was someone profi-
cient in the art of hypnosis. He could have put them
in a trancelike state, shot Edgar Bramwell, then
brought them out of it without anyone remembering
what happened."

"Oh, I see," announced Violet in that snippy way
of hers, "the murderer up and says to one and all in
the middle of a game of charades that he'd like to
hypnotize everyone in the room because there's
some bloke he'd like to murder, thank you very
much. Why," she scoffed, "if I'd of been there I
would have remembered someone wanting to hypnotize me, I would. 'Course, I may be wrong," she
continued in that self-same manner, "but I don't
seem to recollect anyone saying they'd been 'put
under,' so to speak. No, Em, I'm afraid that we'll
just have to roll that idea up along with mine in an
old newspaper and throw it away, in a manner of
speaking, like."

"Hmmm, perhaps. Although I might mention
there is one difference between your theories and
mine that you've overlooked."

"Oh, aye? And what's that then?"

"While your ideas can be explained away as to
why they are not feasible, the hypnosis theory raises
questions. Questions that at this point in time we are
unable to answer. You say you'd remember being
hypnotized. Would you? I wonder. I put it to you,
Mrs. Warner, that it may well be worth our while to
find out what can and cannot be done within the
boundaries of this most intriguing subject."

"Right enough, I suppose," she agreed, albeit
none too convincingly.

"What we need," I stated, "is the advice of an expert in the field."

"Well," she said, after a moment or two of thought, "I could always pop over to me dentist, though I don't like—wait a minute, luv, what about that there American bloke, Mr. Wooley?"

"A good choice," I agreed. "But there's someone else who springs to mind that I believe might be even more knowledgeable."

"Who, then?"

"The Great Zambini."

"The Great Zambini?" was the puzzled response. "And who might he be when he's at home, eh?"

"A professional hypnotist," I replied. "Who, according to our Mr. Wooley, is currently appearing onstage over at the Alhambra. In fact, I might add that the gentleman in question comes highly recommended by Mr. Wooley himself."

"What's the plan, then?" queried Vi in a keen show of interest at the thought of being involved in anything of a theatrical nature.

"I thought perhaps I'd drop over to the theater tonight and see if it's possible to have a little chat with him backstage."

"You?"

"Yes, why?"

"Right, then," was the disgruntled reply. "And I'm to sit here at home by myself twiddlin' me thumbs, am I?"

I was, I admit, quite taken aback by her remark and, as such, quickly responded by informing her that it went without saying that she was perfectly welcome to come along as well.

"You don't think I could handle it on me own

then, is that it?'' she responded, not in a belligerent way, mind you, but I could tell from the hurt in her voice that my two solo outings to the Bramwells' had been a sore spot with her that until now she had kept to herself. ''It's just that I think it would be more fair like, seein' as how we're equal partners and all, if I had a go at it meself,'' she added, in summing up.

Oh, lord, why this time of all times? I mentally asked myself. Any and all information that could be obtained on the subject of hypnosis was too important to be left to—but, perhaps, I thought, I was being too judgmental. After all, if it had not been for her theory of the innocent within the room being drugged, improbable as that idea was, it did, in fact, lead us a step forward. Not that I was all that certain about some sort of hypnotic spell being the solution to the puzzle. But, it was, at least, as Vi would have said, something to hang our hats on.

SIX

Look into My Eyes . . .

I CONTINUED, AS did Vi, to busy myself around the house for the better part of the day with, needless to say, my companion's upcoming visit with the gentleman in question never being far from my thoughts.

As evening at last settled in over the city I accompanied Violet outside the front door to a waiting cab where, after having offered up one last wave, I watched as she set off on her ride to the theater. As the clatter of hoofbeats died out in the distance I reentered the house with a wish that not only would it all go as planned but with a feeling of trepidation as well. Yet, what could go wrong, I asked myself. We had discussed earlier that day what questions should be put to him and if answers led to further questions so much the better. And in the event that the man should take it upon himself to dismiss her

out of hand, we always had Mr. Wooley to fall back
on. Then why, I wondered, did I feel something may
go amiss? Perhaps I was making too much of it. Yes,
that was it. All will go well. All will go well, I repeated in the hope of putting my mind at rest. And,
while I had planned to wait up until her return, as
the night wore on drowsiness overtook me and I
made straight for bed. As such, it was not until the
next morning after I had finished off a plate of kip-
pers and was sipping the last of my tea that Violet,
usually the first to rise, at last entered the kitchen.
"I was just wondering whether to go in and wake
you," I said. "It's not like you to sleep in. Is there
anything that you fancy?"

"A cuppa tea would be fine, luv. If you wouldn't
mind," she answered in between a yawn.

I readied a cup and after placing it before her she
continued to sip away at it while remaining quite
uncommunicative which, for Violet, I thought, was
very odd indeed. Perhaps she'd been unable to arrange a meeting and was hesitant to admit it. If so,
there was only one way to find out. "And how was
your encounter with the great and mysterious Mr.
Zambini?" I asked light-heartedly. "You did see
him, didn't you?" Much to my relief she answered
that she had.

"He'd just finished his act by the time I got there.
Some old geezer backstage took me to his dressing
room to meet him," she added, seemingly non-
plussed by it all. I would have thought she'd be bub-
bling over with excitement.

"Good for you!" I beamed. "What's he like?"

"Who? The old geezer?"

Oh, lord. "No, Vi. Zambini."

"Looked like the devil, he did."

"Dressed shabbily, was he?"

"No, I mean," came the exasperated reply, "he *looked* like the devil. Tall, he is, with black wavy hair and wearing one of them upturned moustaches with a goatee. You know, one of them short, pointy beards. Can't say as how I liked his eyes. Made me nervous they did. Like he could see what I was wearing underneath. Know what I mean?"

"Yes, yes. Go on."

"Gave me his calling card like a right proper gent though, I'll say that for him. And his picture as well. They're on me dresser. Did you see them?"

I admitted that I hadn't. And while I found what she had related so far to be quite fascinating, I was more interested to learn whether she had been able to engage him in conversation with respect to the subject of hypnosis. When I put the question to her I received no answer in return. Instead, she averted her eyes from mine and reset her cup to saucer with a shaking hand. "Is anything wrong?" I asked, noting a now trembling lip. In lieu of an answer, she took me completely by surprise by pushing back her chair and, on rising to a standing position, turned on her heels and made straight for the bedroom. Hesitantly, I followed her in to find her standing with her back to me with shoulders heaving in conjunction with heavy sobbing. "Vi!" I exclaimed, "what on earth's the matter? Is it something I said?"

"Oh, Em," she moaned, burying her face in her hands, "it's not you. It's me! Summat's wrong with me, I just know it."

"There, there," I soothed, gently placing my arm

round her shoulder. "It can't be as bad as all that. What is it that's troubling you?"

"It's me mind," she wailed. "I'm losing me memory, I am. I don't seem to remember whether I asked him any questions or not. But I must have, mustn't I?" she queried in between pitiful sobs. "That's what I went there for, right? But I can't—oh, Em," she moaned, "am I getting old? Is that it?"

I could feel tears welling up in my eyes. "You, getting old?" I responded, drawing her close. "Oh, no, not you, m'girl. The rest of us might be, but not you. Why," I went on, trying to put the best face possible on it, "I daresay it's no more than a case of mental exhaustion. Now then, you get yourself back into bed this very minute, Violet Warner, and don't carry on so. You'll be right as rain before you know it."

After helping her back into bed with an additional word or two of consolement, I picked up the autographed picture and calling card from the dresser top and returned to the kitchen quietly, closing the bedroom door behind me.

What in the world could have come over her? Was I right in thinking it was merely a case of her being overexhausted? Or was it possible, as Violet feared, that senility was setting in? I thought perhaps a nice fresh pot of tea might help me in sorting it all out but, in truth, I was too upset to even bother.

Instead, I sat myself down at the kitchen table and began silently tapping my fingers on the table while picturing in my mind the scene within the dressing room. Or, as much as it was possible to, from what little information Vi had been able to offer up. She enters, no doubt introductions are exchanged. Vi, with all her faculties intact, takes note of the man's appearance. Perhaps it was at this point that he presented his card to her. So far, so good. Now he offers up his picture to her, but wait—wouldn't he have done that when she took her leave? Yes, that seems more plausible. All right, what are we left with then? "A big hole in the middle," I muttered aloud as I continued to drum away on the tabletop. But surely senility, a debilitating disease of the memory bank that occurs gradually over the years, could have played no part in the mystery. And exhaustion? For Violet to have remembered the appearance of the man in detail yet be too "exhausted" to remember whether a conversation had been carried out or not made little or no sense at all.

My finger tapping came to a stop as I idly picked up the man's photograph to find he was as Violet had described him. As I studied the full-face photo I found it to be very dramatic and highly theatrical, with the photographer, by the use of varying degrees of shadow and light, having illuminated the eyes so that they seemed to stare back at the viewer with a singular intensity.

Indeed, as I continued to peer into the picture I felt, if I stared into those eyes long enough, I'd no doubt find myself becoming—wait a minute. "That's it!" I cried aloud. It had to be! I castigated myself for not thinking of it sooner. That horrid man had hypnotized her. It was the only possible explanation. I could accept no other. However, ecstatic though I was on having arrived at the answer, my elation turned sour just as quickly when I realized I hadn't the foggiest idea of why he should have done so. No matter, I told myself, hypnotize her he did. As to the why of it, that could come later. As for now, I believed a little chat with our American neighbor was now in order. As such, I quickly set about jotting down a note to Mr. Wooley with the request that he stop by later that afternoon and had one of the young lads playing outside on the street deliver it. That done, I eagerly awaited Vi's awakening. For which I waited a good two hours before she finally awoke to make her way, still slightly bleary-eyed, from bedroom to kitchen.

No sooner had she sat down than I triumphantly announced that it was my belief that the segment of time missing from her meeting with Zambini was due to his having put her into a hypnotic state. I was, to put it mildly, more than a little surprised (though knowing Vi, I suppose that I shouldn't have been) when she unequivocally rejected the idea.

"What's this you're saying? Hypnotized me? Not ruddy likely," she announced quite adamantly. "Don't believe it for a moment, I don't."

"I see," I responded calmly. "Then we can ascribe your condition to encroaching senility, is that what you're saying?"

" 'Ere," was the flustered reply, "I never said—" She paused, no doubt pondering her choice between senility and being mesmerized. "Well, like as not, you could be right," she at last acquiesced. "I mean, anything's possible, ain't it? But, who knows for certain, eh?"

"Hopefully, Mr. Wooley," I answered.

"Mr. Wooley?"

"I've sent word for him to drop by in the hope

he'll be able to confirm what I believe must have happened.''

By the time the grandfather clock in the parlor had chimed out the second hour of the afternoon the gentleman in question arrived at the front door with hat in hand and looking, as I recall, a trifle perplexed as he brought forth my note from the inside pocket of his badly frayed suit.

"It *was* you that sent this, wasn't it, Mrs. Hudson?" he asked after greetings had been exchanged.

"It was indeed, Mr. Wooley. And I thank you for accepting on such short notice. Come in. Come in."

"Thought it might be somebody playing a joke on me," he admitted on stepping into the vestibule.

"A joke?"

"It's just that it's been awhile," he explained, "since ol' Peter Wooley had what you might call a social invitation."

"Actually," I informed him, "the invitation is more business in nature rather than social. But there's no reason why it couldn't be both," I added with a smile. "Come along, we can talk in the parlor."

"Ah, my hat—?"

"Oh, yes, of course. You can hang it there, if you like," I answered, indicating a tree rack laden down with an assortment of outdoor apparel. "If you can find a spot for it." After locating an empty peg for his woebegone bowler, he paused for a moment, giving close examination to the hat that hung next to it.

"This checkered cloth one here," he asked, "with the front and back flaps, it's what they call a deerstalker cap, isn't it?"

"Yes. I believe so," I answered as I watched him remove it from its peg.

"Well, I swan!" he exclaimed in the sudden realization of what he now held in his hand. "Then this must belong to—"

"It does indeed," I smiled.

"Well, I swan!" he repeated as he continued to hold it reverently in his hands as if it were some kind of religious relic before very carefully replacing it back on its peg.

"Come along, Mr. Wooley," said I, ushering him toward the parlor, "we've business to attend to."

"Lead the way," he answered with one last backward glance at the legendary headgear.

"Please, sit down," I requested of him on entering the room and taking my place beside Vi on the sofa. "You know Mrs. Warner, do you?"

"Just to tip my hat to on the street," he answered with a smile while settling himself down opposite the two of us. "And how are you today, Mrs. Warner?"

"Well enough, I suppose, Mr. Wooley," she answered honestly enough. "All things being equal, as they say. But, what about you, eh? Em here says you were some kind of an entertainer in your day, what with being on the stage, and all. That right?"

"Some kind of an entertainer," he said, repeating the words slowly. "It's not a billing I would have chosen for myself," he added with a deprecating chuckle, "but yes, I suppose you could say I was some kind of an entertainer."

"Don't you rememember, Vi," I spoke up, "seeing Mr. Wooley as Mr. Jolly the Clown when he put on a Christmas show for the children in the church basement last year?''

"Aye, that's right. Laughed ever so much right along with the children, I did.''

"Which, if I'm not mistaken,'' stated the man as a smile emerged from within that worn face, "would be the reason for my visit. There's some such party or other coming up, is there?''

"Actually, no,'' I admitted.

"Oh,'' was the crestfallen reply.

To ease his obvious disappointment I went on to explain that what we sought from him was an insight into what could and couldn't be done within the realm of hypnosis for which, I added, we would gladly reimburse him for any amount he deemed appropriate. And while it was obvious to see simply by his appearance that the man would consider himself fortunate if he had but two farthings to rub together, it was to his credit that he gallantly brushed the idea of any payment aside. However, I insisted, as did Vi, that he be paid for his time, to which he at last reluctantly agreed.

In order for him to fully grasp how important we considered his help in the matter, I set about enlightening him as to our involvement in the Bramwell murder—starting with my visit to Jane Bramwell right up to Vi's backstage encounter with Zambini. As for Mr. Wooley's reaction to all this, he sat for the most part in open-mouthed astonishment until I had at last concluded my narrative.

"Let me get this straight,'' was his somewhat puzzled response as he tried to come to terms with what he had heard. "You say you two ladies are— detectives?''

"In a manner of speaking," answered Vi. "Nothing official, like."

"*Private* detectives," I added.

"And you're working on the Bramwell murder? Why," he exclaimed, "there hasn't been anything as sensational in the papers since the days of Jack the Ripper! If I'd of known of all this when I first came in I'd of hung my hat beside yours, Mrs. Hudson. I surely would," he added, with a hearty slap to his knee.

"Hung his—hat?" queried Vi.

"I'll explain later," I whispered.

"Now then, Mrs. Hudson," spoke our visitor, "what is it exactly that you and Mrs. Warner would like to know?"

"About Vi's missing segment of time," I asked, "is there a chance this Zambini person could have put her into some kind of trance?"

"Against her wishes, you mean?"

"Yes."

Without a moment's hesitation he announced that it would be next to impossible.

My heart sank.

"There, Em, what did I tell you, eh?" wailed Violet. "It's me mind. Going spongy on me, it is. They'll be taking me away one of these days, you'll see."

"Unless . . ." mused Mr. Wooley.

"Yes? Unless what?" I sang out, leaning forward in hopeful expectation.

"Well," he hedged, with a tug or two to his earlobe, "Max is pretty smooth, a real pro, know what I mean? It's just possible he eased her into it before she knew what was happening. That's nothing against you, Mrs. Warner," he was quick to announce. "It's just that, as I say, if anybody could do it, Max could."

"Max?" I queried. "Who in the world is Max?"

"Max Oliver," he replied. "Zambini is just his stage name if we're talking about the same person. Though I don't see how there could be two Zambinis."

"Vi, where's that photograph? I know I brought it in with me earlier."

"Laying right next to you on the table. Right where you put it."

"Oh, yes, so it is. Is this your Max Oliver?" I asked on handing over the Zambini photo to our American friend.

"Yeah, that's him all right," he announced with an admiring glance at the face before him. "Boy, that's some swell picture," he remarked to no one in particular. "Real class. That's Zambini for you."

"Know him then, do you?" asked Vi.

"I know him to say hello to," he answered. "Know others in the business that know him better than I do though."

"And it's your belief," I said, "that this Zambini person or whatever he calls himself, put Mrs. Warner into an hypnotic state. If that's so, it still doesn't—"

"Now, hold on there a minute," he interjected, "I only said it *might* be possible that he could have done it. I didn't say he did."

"That's it then, Em. It's me mind, I knew it," groaned Violet.

"Oh, for heaven's sake, Vi," I snapped, "you're no more losing your mind than I am."

"Than you are, you say? Oh, well, that's all right then, isn't it? And who was it that couldn't remember where she put the photo, eh?"

Thankfully at this point Mr. Wooley stepped in, thereby curtailing any further sniping between two old ladies by announcing there was one way to find out what happened if, as he put it, "Mrs. Warner would be agreeable to a little journey back through time." As he outlined it, it would be a case of re-hypnotizing Vi, as it were, and taking her back in her mind's eye to that moment in time when first she entered the Zambini dressing room to the time she left. "Is such a thing possible?" I asked. And although he readily assured the both of us that it was, Vi, for her part, would have none of it.

I confess I was quite beside myself with her non-acceptance and took it upon myself to ask Mr. Wooley if he would excuse himself from our presence for a minute or two. After he had obligingly shuffled his way out of the room, sliding the door closed behind him, I turned on Vi and demanded to know her reason for dismissing the idea out of hand.

"This hypnotizing business," she answered defensively, "it's spooky, that's what it is. I'll have nowt to do with it."

"Spooky? Spooky?" I exclaimed. "Good heavens, Mrs. Warner, you, of all people, to say it's spooky. And what would you call it when you go 'flitting off' as you say, through doors, walls, and who knows what else?" I questioned, in reference to my companion's ability in being able to release at will her ethereal self from her physical body. And while these out-of-body experiences of hers had, on more than one occasion, proved extremely helpful on previous cases we had collaborated on, it was a secret that we alone shared. Hence my request of Mr. Wooley to indulge Vi and myself in a few minutes of private conversation.

"But that's different," she protested.

"Different? How is it different?"

"When I goes flitting off, *I'm* in control. It's not like I was turning me mind, such as it is, over to somebody else, like."

"Believe me, you've nothing to fear. Mr. Wooley is quite competent. He wouldn't have suggested it otherwise. Besides," I added, "I'll be right there alongside you."

We continued this bantering back and forth for the better part of five minutes until at last a decision was finally reached. I went to the door and, on sliding it open, stepped out to find our visitor once more idly engaged in the examination of a certain item of apparel on the hat rack.

"Oh, Mrs. Hudson, I didn't see you there," was the startled if not somewhat sheepish response. "Has Mrs. Warner—?"

"She's agreed," I announced.

Having received Vi's assurance that she would cooperate fully with him, Mr. Wooley requested of me that I draw the drapes and turn the lamp down to but a flickering glow. Not for theatrical purposes, he informed us, but simply to help in eliminating any outside or undue distraction that may arise. On my having done so, he drew his chair to the front of Vi, who had remained seated on the sofa and, on seating himself down before her, requested that she close her eyes and let herself become completely relaxed. Standing just to the back of Mr. Wooley's chair, I was the recipient of one last look from those questioning eyes before the lids, like the drapes, were quietly closed to the outside world.

He then began a quiet, continuous monotone as to her state of being. Her eyes, he told her, were becoming heavy . . . so heavy . . . so very heavy. Her body felt relaxed . . . so relaxed . . . so very relaxed. She now felt at ease . . . so completely at ease and was conscious now only of his voice. And so it went until minutes later she exhaled a deep sigh and her head fell slightly forward. I found it all utterly fascinating.

"Now that you are completely relaxed, Mrs. Warner," spoke Mr. Wooley in a soothing tone, "I want you to go back in your mind's eye to the time when first you entered the theater." A pause. "You now see yourself backstage, is that correct?"

"Aye," mumbled Vi. "Backstage."

"You are now standing outside Zambini's dressing room door and you feel perfectly relaxed. Now I want you to look straight ahead and tell me what you see."

"A star."

"Pardon?"

"A star. He's got a star on his ruddy door," she answered.

Mr. Wooley and I exchanged silent smiles.

"A star, yes, all right. You're doing fine," he assured her. "Now then, you knock at the door, it opens, and Zambini stands before you. Is that correct?"

Violet shook her head. "No," she answered. "He's calling out for me to come in."

"I see. And you enter?"

"Aye."

"Now tell us, Mrs. Warner, in your own words, what happens next. You'll have no trouble remembering. Everything is crystal clear to you and you continue to feel perfectly relaxed."

"He asks," began Violet, "how I liked the show. I tell him, polite like, that I hadn't seen it and how ever so sorry I was that I hadn't. Ah, he says, then perhaps you're here to engage me to perform at some private function. My card, madam."

"My what?" asked Mr. Wooley, leaning forward, as did I, in trying to catch her words which continued to be delivered in a dull, slightly slurred monotone.

"Card," repeated Vi. "His calling card."

"I see. Go on then, Mrs. Warner."

"I thanks him ever so much but I tell him what I want to know is summat about this here hypnotism business. Oh, he says, thinking of putting an act together, are you? Then he laughs. One of them false laughs like, you know? No, I tell him, you might say it's summat to do with the Bramwell murder, and all."

I winced on hearing what she said, feeling there was no need to bring any mention of our investigation out in the open. Nevertheless, I felt as long as she didn't expand on it in any great detail there could be no real harm in it. Indeed, it would prove to be quite the opposite.

"Continue on, Mrs. Warner, you're doing just fine."

As was he. I found myself quite impressed and yes, perhaps even a little surprised by the very professional manner he exhibited.

"Oh, getting quite upset now, he is," spoke Violet.

"Upset?" questioned Mr. Wooley. "Zambini's upset? Why, what's he saying?"

"He's wanting to know what I have to do with Bramwell's murder. What's your interest in it? Who sent you? he's asking. Raising his voice to me, he is. If you must know, I snaps back, I'm a private investigator. Oh, I'm that riled with him looking down on me in his white tie and tails like he was Mr. High and Mighty. Then you've no real connection with anyone in law enforcement, have you, he asks with a right ugly sneer on his face. A connection with law enforcement? Just Mr. Holmes, I says, if that's what you mean. Holmes? he repeats all upset like. You mean, Sherlock Holmes? I'm nodding, yes."

At this point Vi began chuckling quietly away to herself. "What is it?" I asked, taking my place beside her on the sofa. "What's happening?"

"Mrs. Hudson would like to know what you find so amusing, Mrs. Warner," intereceded Mr. Wooley. "You may answer her."

"Oh, Em, you should see his face when I mentions Mr. Holmes's name. Standing there, he is, with his mouth hanging open and looking all flustered like."

I managed for Vi's sake, lest I wake her prematurely, to somehow control my excitement on all that I had heard. For this Zambini person to react in such a manner not only to Vi's mention of the Bramwell murder but to his outright display of panic at the thought that she or, for that matter Sherlock Holmes himself (mistaken though he was on that score), was involved in the investigation that he believed had led directly to his door, could mean only one thing.

If it was nothing but sheer luck, rather than any brilliant deduction on my part, that we had the good fortune to stumble across the one man in London, outside of our circle of suspects, who was in some way or other connected to the murder, then so be it. I was not one, as the saying goes, to look a gift horse (or hypnotist) in the mouth.

"What do you see happening now?" asked Mr. Wooley.

"He's turned his back on me," she answered. "Standing there, he is, staring into the mirror and not saying a word. Like he's thinking 'bout summat."

"And you are—?"

"Wondering whether to leave or not. Wait—he's turning round now and asking, nice as you please, my pardon for his behavior. Saying as how his nerves are always jangled like, after putting on a show. Now he's offering me a chair. What's his game, eh? That's what I'm wondering. So I sets meself down. Now he's pouring himself a drink and offering me one. Care to join me? he asks. No, I says, I'll have nowt. Thanks all the same, I'm sure."

"And quite right you were, too," I stated.

"Did I mention before that he talks funny, like?" she added.

"Funny?" Mr. Wooley and I exchanged a puzzled glance but let it pass. I was more perplexed by the fact that she hadn't remembered anything of what she was now telling us when she arrived home—and I questioned Mr. Wooley as to why that would be.

"Can't say as how I know," he answered. "Strange, though, that's for sure. Should we continue on?" he asked. "I don't like to keep her under too long. Though she seems to be holding up. How are you feeling, Mrs. Warner?" he asked in a most solicitous manner.

"Right as rain and twice as nice," she answered, as only Vi could.

"I think it's safe to carry on," I smiled.

Under Mr. Wooley's gentle prodding, Violet told how Zambini turned the conversation back to the art of hypnosis by bringing forth from his jacket pocket a small, beautiful cut-glass pendant on a silver chain, which he then exhibited to her.

"It's all quite simple, really, he's telling me," she stated. "He's saying one just swings it back and forth like, in front of the subject's eyes."

"And is that what he's doing now?" I questioned. "Swinging it back and forth in front of your eyes?"

"Aye. Oh, Em," she suddenly blurted out, "you should see it, you should. All colors of the rainbow it has when it catches the light just right. What you do, he's telling me, is keep repeating how at ease the subject is and how relaxed they feel."

"And no doubt," I responded with a woeful shake of my head, "that is now what he's telling *you*."

"Aye—that's—right. Got—to—remember—all—this," she mumbled, as she continued to drag out each word until whatever else she said was lost to us as she became less and less coherent. Then, dead silence.

"Vi!" I cried out. "Are you all right? Mr. Wooley, what's happening?"

"He's put her under," he smiled, in obvious admiration for his fellow performer. "Didn't I tell you he's a real pro?"

"That may be all very well and good," I shot back, now more angry than upset, "but what of Mrs. Warner?"

"There now, Mrs. Hudson," he announced reassuringly, "there's no need to worry. Mrs. Warner," he asked, on returning his attention to her slumped figure on the sofa, "can you hear me?"

After a prolonged silence, a feeble "Aye" was ushered up, to which I breathed a heartfelt sigh of relief.

"Now then, Mrs. Warner," continued Mr. Wooley, "I want you to take a deep breath—that's right. That relaxes you, doesn't it. Yes, you're feeling quite relaxed now as you remain seated on your chair in the Zambini dressing room. He's standing there before you. He's speaking to you, is that right?"

"Aye, that's right," she admitted after a moment's pause.

"Tell us what he's saying to you, Mrs. Warner. Could you do that for us?"

"He's saying he wants me to do a little favor for him. Says we all enjoy doing favors for people, don't we? Says it's quite simple, really. All I want you to do, he's saying, is to blot out from your mind all that we have said. You'll remember nothing save for coming into my dressing room and my handing you my card. The time in between is a blank to you. It's been all washed away. You'll remember nothing. Nothing at all. Do you understand? Aye, I says. What do you remember, he asks? I remember coming in, I mumbles. Go on, he says, and what else?

You gave me your card, I answer. And what else? Nothing else, I says. Good, very good. He's smiling now."

"Anything else, Vi?" I asked.

"He's saying if Mr. Holmes should ask whether the Great Zambini is in any way involved in the death of Edgar Bramwell, I'm to tell him there's absolutely no connection. And that my coming here was no more than a wild goose chase. Mr. Holmes? I says, don't know as how he'd be asking me, I tell him. Oh, I'm sure he will when you report back to him, he says. He's got me all muddled, he has."

"Is there anything else you can tell us?" questioned Mr. Wooley.

"He's saying," she went on after emitting a deep sigh, "that he's going to count to ten backwards and then I'll awake remembering nothing but what he told me. And that I'd feel as fresh as a morning in May."

"And did you?"

"Aye, I suppose I did."

"And, on waking—?"

"I stand up, we shake hands, and he tells me how much he enjoyed our little visit and would I like his autographed picture. Oh, I says, that would be ever so nice. Then he signs it, hands it to me, and shows me to the door like a real gentleman and off I go. Still can't say as how I liked his eyes, though."

"I think that should do it, Mrs. Hudson," stated Mr. Wooley. "Unless there's something else you'd like to ask her."

"No, no, nothing else," I answered with a smug, satisfied smile. For with Zambini's added reference to Mr. Holmes, there could now be no doubt that he had indeed played a part in the mystery. Whether he was the actual murderer or simply a pawn I had no way of knowing. Nevertheless, I could take some small measure of satisfaction in the knowledge that we had advanced a considerable distance in our journey toward the truth.

Mr. Wooley then set about returning Vi to consciousness by more or less following the same procedure as had Zambini. The one exception being his repeated announcements that this time she would, on waking, remember all that she had related to us. As her eyes fluttered open, I must say it did my heart good to see the overwhelming sense of relief she exhibited in the realization that it was not the symptons of advancing age but the master hypnotist himself who had been the cause of her lapse in memory.

"Would you say, from what you know of this Max Oliver or Zambini or whatever he calls himself," I asked of Mr. Wooley, "that he is a man who would be party to a murder—if not commit the deed himself?"

"Who, Max!" he exclaimed. "You gotta be kidding. Don't let his photo there fool you. I'll admit he looks pretty intimidating, but from what I hear, he's all bluster with the backbone of a jellyfish. Remember how Mrs. Warner said he acted when she mentioned the name of Sherlock Holmes?"

"Aye," confirmed Vi. "I can see him now, I can, quaking in his boots. He's guilty of summat, and no mistake."

"But murder?" Mr. Wooley shook his head. "The only killing he'd like to make is at the race track. Great one for the horses, they tell me. As well, they say, for being a sucker for any so-called get-

rich-quick scheme that comes along. But murder?''
he repeated. ''I just can't see it. Still, you never
know, do you?''

''In any event,'' I stated, ''it goes without saying
that the man warrants a return visit.''

''Well, you can count me out,'' announced Vi in
no uncertain words. ''Had me fill of him, I have.''

''If you'd like *me* to come along—''

''Thank you, no, Mr. Wooley,'' I answered. ''It
is my intention to see this 'Great Zambini' for myself and by myself.''

SEVEN

Mr. Burke Drops By

AFTER A POT of tea had been consumed, hot buttered scones devoured, and a profusion of thank you's offered up by both Vi and myself, Mr. Wooley, on rising to take his leave, assured me that if on some future occasion I felt he could be of further service I was not to hesitate to call upon him at any time of the night or day. As I could not rule out such a possibility, I was quick to say I would take him up on his offer.

Having exchanged my last farewell with him on the outside stoop, I paused before reentering the house to see him saunter off down the street with, I might add, a decided swagger to his step. He must have sensed I had him under observation for he turned round, saw me, tipped his hat and, after an exaggerated bow from the waist, did a little two-step (much to the amusement of myself and of those passing by) before once more proceeding jauntily on his way, obviously quite pleased with himself. As well he should have been.

"I don't suppose there's any need now for the drapes to be drawn," I mentioned to Vi on my return to the parlor. "If you want to see to it, I'll tidy up these empty cups and plates and take them back to the kitchen." On noting there was but one remaining scone left uneaten, I asked Vi whether or not she wanted it.

She shook her head. "Don't want to spoil me supper. Should have given it to Mr. Wooley if we'd of thought of it."

"Actually," I smiled, "I saw him quietly put one or two in his coat pocket when he thought no one was watching."

"Poor ol' bloke," she sighed. " 'Ere, gave him his money, did you?"

"Yes, at the door."

"Can't say as how he didn't deserve it. Why," she said, "if it hadn't of been for him, and me as well for that matter, we'd of never of known this here Zambini person had summat to do with the Bramwell murder."

She and Mr. Wooley? I was cut to the quick. Nevertheless, in measured tones I coolly replied how fortunate it was that I had the foresight to send for Mr. Wooley in the first place. My feelings and my response were not lost on her.

"Oh, aye, well," she flustered, "I'm not saying you don't deserve some credit, like, Em." Anything further either one of us might have added was cut short by a sudden and most unexpected deafening bang from outside.

"What on earth!" I exclaimed as we rushed in tandem to the window.

As Vi hastily drew back the drapes we saw the object that had instigated the noise had not been a bomb, which had been my first thought, but rather a very large automobile that had pulled up to an abrupt stop just outside.

"Why, it's one of them newfangled motor carriages," announced Vi. "It's a wonder it didn't give half the horses on Baker Street a heart attack," she added derisively at this latest mode of transportation that was ever increasingly making itself felt and heard throughout the streets of London.

"It backfired," I said.

"It did what?"

"Backfired," I repeated. "That's what the noise was."

"Whatever would it do that for?"

"I haven't the foggiest," I confessed. "But according to Mr. Hawkins, the blacksmith, that's what they do from time to time."

"Well, they can say what they want about 'em," stated my companion most emphatically, "but mark my words, Emma Hudson, they'll never replace the horse."

"Time will tell, as they say," was my noncommittal reply.

In our continued stance from behind the curtain we watched as two men emerged from either side of the machine.

"No doubt they're here to see Mr. Holmes," remarked Vi peering out round my shoulder.

"Then they're here without an appointment," I answered. "If you recall, both Mr. Holmes and Doctor Watson left word they—wait a minute, he looks somewhat familiar.''

"Who? The one wearing the cap and the funny goggles?''

"No,'' I answered, parting the muslin-curtained window the better to see, "the other chap. Yes, it is, it's Mr. Burke. And the other man, the driver, is Martin.''

"Aye, it's them all right,'' confirmed Violet, stepping up a little closer to the window. " 'Ere,'' she added with an impish grin and a nudge to my side, "won't this give the neighbors summat to talk about, eh? I mean, being called upon by a gentleman in a motor carriage and all.''

"No doubt they'll believe his business is with Mr. Holmes,'' I replied. "Which, in any event, is just as well.''

Vi was beside herself. "Emma Hudson,'' she castigated me, "you vex me summat fierce, you do! Don't you ever want to fluff up your feathers and be the Queen Bee just for once?''

"One celebrated individual within this household is quite enough, thank you very much,'' I answered. To which my companion shook her head in a display of utter despair at this ongoing desire of mine for preferred anonymity.

By this time, Martin had produced a large white cloth from somewhere or other and was now in the act of very lovingly running it over the car's bonnet in little circular motions. Mr. Burke, for his part, had taken leave of Martin and was heading toward the premises of 221B Baker Street.

"I wonder what he wants with us?'' questioned

Vi on making her way from parlor to front door in anticipation of his arrival.

In words to that effect, it was the very question I put to him myself after perfunctory greetings had been exchanged on his entrance and he had settled himself, as best as possible, into the chair opposite the two of us on the sofa. In hindsight, I should have offered him the sofa for he was a big man who looked slightly uncomfortable as he shifted his weight about in a quest for the perfect position for both himself and those great gangling legs of his.

As to my question, he answered that he had earlier called upon Mrs. Bramwell to inquire of that lady whether she knew what progress, if any, had been made by either the Yard or myself. "On learning that she had not heard from you of late," he continued, "I offered to pop over here myself. And here I am, by Jove."

"Yes," I smiled, "we were made all too aware of your arrival."

"What? Oh, the motor car, you mean. Yes, they do tend to be a trifle noisy at times, don't they. But Mrs. Bramwell, dear lady that she is, was thoughtful enough to put both it and Martin at my disposal. So there you are."

"Well, what's the lad doing outside?" queried Vi. "Should have asked him in. We don't stand on ceremony round here."

"I did ask him, actually," he answered. "Seems he'd rather spend what time he has on polishing the car. Can't say as how I blame him. It's quite a beauty, wouldn't you say, Mrs. Warner?"

"Hmmm," murmured Vi, mustering up at best a faint but diplomatic smile.

Evidently her response satisfied him for he returned the smile before plunging on. "Now then, as you two ladies have no doubt noticed," he began, "the papers have been downplaying the murder as of late. I take it by that, the public's interest in it is waning. And about jolly well time, too. All this nonsense about an invisible man." His face registered disgust.

"Can't blame the papers though," spoke Vi. "Didn't have all that much to go on, did they? By way of facts, I mean."

"Does that make it right that they should present us to the public as idiots?" he shot back. "And our lives made an open book to any man with a penny for a paper? This whole thing has completely destroyed my credibility," he carried on in much the same manner. "And, I might add, my chances for ever procuring the necessary funds here in England for my lost mine expedition."

"Yes," I agreed, "I could see that it would. But, as to your meeting with Mrs. Bramwell, has she herself any idea as to the Yard's progress?"

"She says not," he answered, drawing his legs up. "That inspector chap—what's his name?"

"MacDonald."

"Yes, that's it. Say's she hasn't seen or heard from him. Makes one wonder."

"As to—?"

"Whether they've given up on the case," he replied. "No doubt they're hoping somehow it will all fade away into oblivion. Oh, I know," he added, on seeing I was about to interject, "they always say the files remain open on any unsolved murder. But what does that mean? I mean, really. Just pap for the public, if you ask me.''

I put it to him that what it means is that should any clue or useful information come their way, be it next week or next year, it will be acted upon immediately. Thus, the open file, in effect, is an ongoing investigation. Though not necessarily one on a day-to-day basis. "In any event," I added, "you can be sure the Yard is working day and night to clear up the mystery of *this* most singular and baffling murder."

"Can I indeed?" was the disgruntled reply. "The thing of it is, Mrs. Hudson, I, and the others as well, are still under orders and I say 'orders' though the inspector would prefer it phrased as a 'request' that we remain in London until there's an end to this whole infernal mess. And who can say how long that will be?"

"Itching to get back to Africa, are you?" asked Vi.

"I'm itching, as you say, Mrs. Warner, to cross the channel. I have a number of contacts in the various capitals of Europe that I could see with regard to the financing of the expedition."

"Ah, yes, as to this expedition of yours, I believed you mentioned Edgar Bramwell had agreed to put up the money before his untimely death, didn't you?" I asked and, as I did, I studied him most intensely as to how he would respond, knowing that Jane Bramwell had told me the exact opposite was true.

"I did indeed, Mrs. Hudson. I did indeed. If it hadn't have been for that fatal shot I'd be sailing halfway down the Suez by now."

Well, there it was. My first impression was that it had been too quick an answer—as if it had been rehearsed. And there *had* been an avoidance of eye contact but, then again, that could be neither here nor there. And yet—at that point, my thoughts were put on hold by his putting a question to me.

"Mrs. Hudson," he queried, "if you don't mind me asking, what progress if any have *you* ladies made? Any clues or leads? That sort of thing, as they say."

"Oh, aye," spoke Vi before I had a chance to respond. "We've got what you might call a lead. Leastways, more'n what Scotland Yard has, I'll wager. 'Course," she added in a smug little smile, "I don't mind telling you it were all due to me. What with me being put 'under' so to speak, by—"

"Vi!" I cried out, cutting her off. Oh, I was livid. My eyes shot daggers at her.

Vi, realizing her gaffe, looked mortified. Mr. Burke, puzzled. And I, knowing I had to come up with some sort of explanation, did my best to assure the man that what my companion had meant was that our ongoing investigation had put her "under" a bit of a strain of late. As it had myself, I added, galloping along in a rush of words in the hope of somehow making it all sound plausible. True, I told him, we had been fortunate enough through it all to have come up with a lead but where it would take us we had no way of knowing.

While he still appeared to be left a little puzzled, much to my relief it did seem he accepted my garble of words at face value. But what of later? Would Vi's utterance of being "put under" register with him as pertaining to a foray into hypnotism? And if it did? There'd be no harm if he was not the guilty party. But as to that, we had no way of knowing. Still, if he was completely free of any wrongdoing, there was still the chance he could innocently enough pass along the incident of Vi's faux pas to the one that was. What a mess. Any hope that I had put an end to it was dashed when he questioned me as to what the lead was of which I had spoken.

I winced. "Mr. Burke," I answered, "you put me in an awkward position. You must realize you are still, how shall I say—"

"A suspect? Yes, yes, I see what you mean," he replied, shifting his weight about. "Forgive me, Mrs. Hudson, but you can understand my curiosity under the circumstances."

"Only too well," I replied. "It's best we say no more about it. Now then, as to the others you spoke of earlier, the MacPhails, Mr. Moore, Miss Armstrong-Jones, you've seen them recently, have you?"

"No, not I, but Jane—Mrs. Bramwell, did mention she'd been in contact with them once or twice. You did know that Moore and his fiancée are staying two doors down, didn't you?"

"Two doors down? I'm afraid I don't understand."

"From the Bramwells," he explained. "Seems Miss Armstrong-Jones's great aunt, Mrs. Hamilton, has her residence there—it being but one of her many homes both here and abroad from what I understand."

Violet was aghast. "You don't mean to say the two of them are staying in the same house together!" she exclaimed, thereby breaking her silence by no doubt feeling she'd done penance enough by maintaining it for as long as she had since that last unfortunate outburst of hers.

"It's not exactly a country cottage in Devon, Mrs. Warner," he smiled. "It does have a large number of guest rooms and what with Mrs. Hamilton being the woman she is—I attended one of her musicales there at one time. It was all rather dull as was the lady herself, as I recall," he added in an aside. "You can rest assured that all the rules of propriety will be strictly adhered to."

Violet was relieved. "Oh, well, that's all right then, I suppose. But why are they—?"

"Staying there? As a matter of convenience, I would imagine. Being both from Manchester it does solve the problem for them on where to stay while in London; what with the inspector wanting to keep us all at his beck and call, as it were. And from what Mrs. Bramwell tells," he added, "they are all as anxious as I to have this wretched affair wrapped up as quickly as possible."

"As do Mrs. Warner and myself," I assured him.

"We live in hope do we not, Mrs. Hudson."

"We do indeed, Mr. Burke."

"And on that note, ladies," he stated on bringing himself out of the chair, "I shall take my leave. Oh, by the way," he added as we walked him to the door, "there is one little incident I could pass along to you for whatever it may be worth."

"Oh, aye, and what would that be, then?" questioned Vi.

"Seems the MacPhails were seen by the inspector emerging from a Cunard shipping lines office the other day," he answered. "Hello, hello, what's this then? says the inspector. Not thinking of leaving

London just yet by sailing off for parts unknown, are you? To which MacPhail replies that they were just in pricing passage fares to pass the time of day. Just for a lark, he adds, nothing more. Well, now, says the inspector, larks have a habit of flying off, don't they? And, he says, we wouldn't want you two flying the coop just yet, would we? It would appear that," chuckled our visitor, "the inspector is the possessor of a cutting if not a dry wit."

"Yes, but as to the MacPhails—how do you know all this?" I asked.

"A fellow member over at the club knows one or two chaps down at the Yard and, well, one does hear things over a drink or two. Or three or four, for that matter," he quipped.

"And I thought it was just we women who loved to gossip," I added with a smile.

"Not so," was his light-hearted reply. "The difference between the sexes on that score being that the female of the species have no need for alcoholic stimuli to set their tongues a-wagging. Now then," he added before either I or Violet had a chance to respond, "I really must be off."

As we bid him good day, I thought to ask if he'd be good enough to inform Mrs. Bramwell on his arrival that I'd be in touch with her in no more than a day or two. On his assurance that he would indeed do so, he exited, thanking us both in turn for our having received him.

"Oh, Em, it's that sorry I am for blurting out— you know what. Whatever must you think?" groaned my companion with a wringing of her hands as we reentered the parlor.

"That in trying to impress the gentleman," I replied, "you spoke first without thinking. But, never mind old girl, it's all over and done with now," I added, for which I was the recipient of a small but relieved sigh. "But, 'ere, now," she carried on, "why do you suppose he came snooping round here looking for information, eh?"

"I think you've just answered your own question," I replied. "If Mr. Burke is an innocent in all this, it's understandable that he'd want to know what's going on."

"And if he's guilty?"

"All the more reason, wouldn't you say?"

"It's summat to think about."

"Isn't it?"

Violet pondered the thought for a moment or two and, obviously reaching no conclusion one way or the other wondered aloud what I thought of Mr. Burke's story regarding the MacPhails. "Think it's true, do you?" she asked.

Before answering I paused in the parting of the curtains to view the Bramwell motor car take off in a cloud of blue smoke down Baker Street. "What? Oh, the MacPhails?" I replied, turning back from the window. "Do I think it's true? Yes, I imagine it is. At least the fact that they were seen leaving the shipping office. Mr. Burke knows only too well we could seek verification of his story from the inspector. Though, if the two of them were thinking of leaving the country it would look very bad for them indeed. Still, it could very well have been just as they say—something to do to pass the time of day. A dreamer's holiday, no more, no less. I've done the same thing myself, if truth be known," I confessed, thinking back to the time of my husband's passing and of wanting to free myself from a world that had collapsed around me. But, in the realization that there is no shore distant enough in which to hide from oneself, I was obliged to carry on with life as best I could.

"What? Done the same thing yourself, you say? When was all this, then?"

"It was—a long time ago. Now then, Mrs. Warner," said I, in seeking to bring the subject to a close, "I'd say it was high time we saw to our supper. Then it's an early night for me if I'm to have my wits about me for tomorrow."

"What's on the agenda for tomorrow, then?"

"First off," I answered, "I thought I'd pay a call on Mr. Moore. He seems to be a shadowy figure at best in all this. I'd like to flesh him out—you know, get a better handle on him, so to speak. I don't think I'll bother to send my calling card in advance. Might be best if I just pop over and take my chances of being admitted. You're welcome to come along, of course," I added. "No," she answered, "I'll pass on that one if you don't mind. Might put me foot in it again by saying summat I oughtn't."

I breathed a sigh of relief but, for appearances' sake, I pooh-poohed such an idea and again repeated the offer; thankfully, she once more declined.

"You said 'first off,' where else then?" she questioned.

"After seeing Mr. Moore, which hopefully I will," I answered, "I'm off to the theater."

"The theater?"

"To have a word or two with your friend, the 'Great Zambini,' " I teased.

"*My* friend, is he? I like that, I do!" she huffed.

"Like I told you before, Em, I've had my fill of him, I have. And it's quite welcome you are to see him on your own, I'm sure. But, mind, you best be on your toes. He's a tricky one, he is, and no mistake."

"I'll keep my eyes open for any swinging pendants," I answered with a smile. But for all my bravado, I had mixed emotions regarding the upcoming encounter—an eagerness to find out just what his involvement in the murder was and a feeling of trepidation regarding the actual meeting itself. "As for now," I added, "let's see about supper, shall we?"

"You're not thinking about toad-in-the-hole again, are you?" questioned Vi, making a face.

"If I am," I responded in what I deemed a frosty tone, "it will be done with the required ingredients."

"*Two* eggs, you mean then, right?"

What was I to do with her?

EIGHT

The Great Zambini

꧁I RAPPED ONCE, waited, then rapped again and, in the waiting, I heard the sound of someone fumbling with the lock from inside. As the door finally swung open, I was confronted by a pretty young thing in maid's dress. "This *is* the Hamilton residence, isn't it?" I asked. For a while I remembered Mr. Burke had stated it was but two doors down from the Bramwells'; I hadn't thought to ask in what direction. She nodded in the affirmative, stating that indeed it was. "I'm Mrs. Hudson," I said, introducing myself with a smile. "I'd like to see Mr. Moore, if I may."

"Oh, I'm sorry," was her apologetic response, "but I'm afraid Mr. Moore isn't receiving any—"

"Who is it, Bessie?" questioned a voice from within, which I instantly recognized as being that of Miss Armstrong-Jones.

"A lady to see Mr. Moore—a Mrs. Hudson," she answered, turning her head slightly in the direction of the voice. "I've told her that—"

"That's all right, Bessie," stated the woman as she came into view. "I'll see to it. Mrs. Hudson," she beamed on catching sight of me, "come in. Come in."

"Miss Armstrong-Jones, how are you?" I asked on entering. "I apologize for turning up so unexpectedly but I was just passing by and—"

"Just 'passing by,' you say?" she questioned with a good-humored smile.

I'd been caught in a white lie, for we both knew I'd no more be passing by such a prestigious address as would she in taking a stroll down Baker Street. "Well, in point of fact," I confessed, "I did actually make the trip specifically to see Mr. Moore. Have I arrived at a bad time? You've eaten, have you?"

"*I* have, yes," she answered. "Though, in truth, our meals of late have no set schedule. My great aunt, being a woman of advanced years and not in the best of health, has confined herself to her room where she eats, sleeps, and nothing much else, I'm afraid. As for dear Mr. Moore, he's been off his food for some time and eats at no particular hour of the night or day. He's—he's not been well, you see."

"I'm sorry to hear that," I responded politely enough. "What is it that ails him?"

"I put it down to depression, Mrs. Hudson."

"Depression?"

"Yes, I believe it has to do with all this murder business," she confided. "He's not been the same since it happened. Then again, who has, I ask you? Still, what with losing his position and being placed under a cloud of suspicion in the death of Mr. Bramwell—"

"He does not stand alone under that cloud," I interjected.

"What? Oh, yes, I see what you mean. But what people don't seem to realize about poor Arthur is that he is quite a sensitive man, really, for all his bluff ways."

"And you say you believe this is the reason for his state of mental health? You've not spoken to him directly about this yourself?"

"No, not really. Well, you see," she added in noting my surprise at this apparent lack of communication between the two of them, "I thought it best not to speak of anything of an unpleasant nature with the thought in mind it might upset him even more. I like everything to be nice, you see. It upsets me just knowing that he's upset. But you spoke of wanting to see him. You have news, do you?"

"No, not really," I admitted. "I just thought— perhaps," I added as an afterthought, "my visit was ill-timed. If, as you say, he's not up to receiving visitors, another time might be more convenient." With my recollection of Mr. Moore as someone whom I would not consider to be the most affable of men at the best of times, I did not relish the thought of engaging him in conversation if, as Prudence Armstrong-Jones had informed me, he was in a state of deep melancholy.

"Nonsense," she announced, cupping her hand under my elbow and ushering me along. "I'd say you arrived at a most opportune time. Perhaps this is what he needs—someone to talk it out with, as it were. They do say it's easier to confide in a stranger than a loved one. But why that should be I'm sure I don't know. He's in the drawing room—this way," she added while continuing to ramble on until we at last arrived at a most elegantly appointed, high-ceilinged, chandeliered room. "Arthur," she said, addressing the man somewhat timidly as we entered, "it's Mrs. Hudson. She's come to pay you a visit."

"Has she indeed, by gad," grumbled the slumped figure in the chair without bothering to rise or offer up so much as a how-do-you-do.

Miss Armstrong-Jones appeared embarrassed. "Now, Arthur," she soothed, "do be nice."

"Come to arrest me, have you, Mrs. Hudson?" he inquired sarcastically with but a cursory glance in my direction.

"Now then, Mr. Moore," I answered lightly, lest he think his manner had the effect of intimidating me, "you know I don't have the authority to arrest anyone."

"And Scotland Yard," he went on, ignoring my response, "surrounded the house, have they?"

"Oh, Arthur," pleaded the woman, "must you carry on so?"

He turned on her with a withering stare but said nothing, his silence all the more terrible for it. "Ah, yes, well, I'll—I'll just leave you two alone for a bit then, shall I?" she stammered while in the process of withdrawing herself from the room.

"And I'll sit down then, shall I?" I asked on her departure.

"If you are so inclined, madam," he answered wearily with a wave of his hand toward the chair to the front of him.

"Now what's all this business about Scotland

Yard and my arresting you?" I asked on settling myself down. "Am I right in thinking it as being nothing more than a facetious remark on your part?"

"Take it any way you will."

"Come now, Mr. Moore," I reasoned, "this state you've got yourself into will do you no good. You are but one on a list of suspects."

"And I'm to take comfort in that, am I?" he snapped. "It wasn't bad enough when rumors of my so-called incompetence as a businessman were spread about but then, to be included as a suspect in the Bramwell murder—" He lowered his head and with eyes set fixedly on the floor, emitted a deep sigh. "Where will it all end?" he asked after an interval of prolonged silence. I had no answer. Nor did I think one was expected of me. "Perhaps a glass of port will set things right," he said, mustering up a faint smile as he shifted his weight about toward the decanter placed on the table to his left. "Will you join me, Mrs. Hudson?" I shook my head no. He poured a drink for himself, took a small mouthful, and reset the glass. "If this whole thing were cleared up tomorrow," he carried on, "with the guilty party shouting his confession from the rooftops of London, I would still be singled out by my colleagues as 'the chap who was somehow involved in the death of Edgar Bramwell.' He who steals my purse steals trash but he who steals my name—well, you get my meaning."

"As to these accusations about your drinking and the financial decline of the company over the last few years," I asked, "you say it is nothing but—?"

"Nonsense—stuff and nonsense!" he thundered, at last breaking out of his lethargy. "And I can assure you, Mrs. Hudson, if I were not in the company of a lady my denouncement would be much more explicit!''

I made no reply other than to direct my attention to the glass of port that sat beside him. He took my meaning. ''Well, of course, I drink,'' he stated. ''What man doesn't, eh? But not to the extent our Mr. Bramwell would have had you believe. You speak of company profits—or loss of them. Aye, I'll admit we have had a few bad years as does every business. But we were never in the red.''

''Then why—?''

''Get the old man out—that was young Bramwell's plan. Bring in new blood, that sort of thing. He couldn't fire me outright, it wouldn't sit well with some of the more senior members of our club. Nor did he want to ostracize himself within the business community. Of which,'' he added, with no little pride, ''I came highly respected. So rumors were started about my so-called drinking habits and how I was pulling the company down around me.'' He reached for his port, then for some reason or the other, thought better of it and set it back down.

''But you didn't kill him, is that what you're saying?''

''I'm glad he's dead,'' he answered.

''And what of Miss Armstrong-Jones?'' I asked. ''What are your feelings toward her in all this?''

''Pru's a good old soul,'' he smiled wistfully. ''She means well.''

''Means well? Good heavens man, she loves you.''

''Aye,'' he answered after a moment or two of

thought. "I suppose she does. As do I her. But if you're speaking of marriage—"

"I am."

"Perhaps—if the word pity were to be included in the vows."

Oh, that man exasperated me. "Do you think," I railed, "she feels nothing more for you than pity?"

He returned to his vigil of eyeing some imaginary spot on the floor and offered up no reply. Very well then, if he wanted to wallow in his own misery then so be it. As he had nothing more to say and as there was nothing more to be said, I rose, wished him an obligatory good night, and took my leave.

On stepping out into the hallway, I was met by a waiting and anxious Prudence Armstrong-Jones. "What did he say?" she inquired of me, her face searching mine for some word of encouragement. What could I tell her? I thought for a moment. "He said," I answered, "he said he loves you." Which was true enough. That plain but loving face broke into a wreath of smiles.

With that, I bid her a good evening and, once outside, hailed a cab with instructions I be taken to the Alhambra theater.

Well, Emma Hudson, I asked myself as the cabbie set off at a smart pace, what did you learn, if anything, from your visit with Mr. Arthur Moore? That he was in a depressed state there was no doubt. That was no act put on for my benefit. But if life's rug had pulled out from under him, was he himself to blame or was he merely an innocent who had the misfortune to have been caught in someone else's web?

One could say that Bramwell's death had only

made it worse for him. Prior to the murder he was without position, his reputation damaged, and plans for a forthcoming marriage put on hold. The last thing he needed was to be even remotely suspected in the death of the man he held responsible for his present circumstances. Then again, one could make the argument that being in a depressed state with revenge being first and foremost on his mind he committed the deed without thinking through what the future consequences of his action would be. As one can see, there are two sides to every coin. And this particular coin, I'm afraid, would have to be deposited in my memory bank until a more opportune time presented itself. As for now, I had other thoughts to occupy my mind, namely, my meeting with the Great Zambini.

On arriving at the theater I bypassed the entrance and made my way down a narrow alley to the side of the building, where I found the stage door unlocked. I timidly pushed it open and entered into another world.

A parade of people including some scantily clad ladies of the chorus were rushing madly about in all directions while orders were being barked out by someone, somewhere, over the sound of the orchestra tuning up out front. The curtains were drawn and the area was badly lit, but I began to make my way forward, being mindful not to become entangled in the rigging of ropes that hung down from the blackness above when a raspy voice sang out.

"Oy, you there, missus. You're not allowed back here."

The voice belonged to a spindly old duffer seated

behind a small wooden desk as rickety as the man himself.

"I'm here to see Mr. Zambini," I said, stopping in my tracks to address him.

"Zambini? Expecting you then, is he?"

"Yes," I lied.

"You've a name then, have you?" was the snide little remark I received from the old man who obviously enjoyed his position as guardian of the stage door.

"A name? Of course I have a name," I answered, somewhat put off by his high-handed manner. "It's Hudson. Mrs. Hudson."

He removed a rolled sheet of paper from the pigeon-holed top of his desk and held it up but an inch or two from his eyes before at last announcing that he had no Mrs. Hudson listed.

"Obviously you weren't informed," I blithley replied while wondering how in the world Vi had been lucky enough to have gotten by him on her visit.

"It wouldn't be the first time," he grumbled. "Security is always the last to know. You're sure he's expecting you? He already has visitors," he added, returning the paper to its slot.

"He has? Well, then, one more won't matter will it? Of course you could always check with Mr. Zambini yourself," I bluffed.

"You're here now, best you go on ahead," he answered after a moment or two of thought. Obviously the idea of having to stir himself from his chair didn't sit all that well with him—if I may be permitted a small pun.

"And where would I find him?" I asked.

A spasm of coughing and wheezing followed before he at last answered, "Stage left."

"Stage—?"

"That way," he answered, pointing a bony, tobacco-stained finger. " 'Cross the stage then turn left. You'll see his door. And be quick about it, mind," he added, "if you don't want to find yourself halfway 'cross the stage when the curtain goes up."

As I had no wish in making a theatrical debut on this or any other stage, I scurried over, catching the sound of the audience filing in down the aisle as I did so. Once on the other side, I had no trouble spotting the door emblazoned with a star just as Vi had described it in her trancelike state. On making my way forward I noticed the door suddenly open to allow three matronly ladies to emerge. No doubt the visitors the old gentleman had spoken about. Framed within the doorway stood the man himself, whom I recognized from Violet's photograph of him.

"Oh, Mr. Zambini," gushed one of the three, a plump, overdressed woman in her fifties, "I can't tell you how thrilled we are that you found time to see us."

"And thank you ever so much for your picture," cooed the second lady.

"And for signing it and all," added the third.

"*You* thank *me?* It is zee Great Zambini who thanks *you*, dear ladies," he answered, speaking of himself in the third person. "Now run along, my little ones, or you'll miss the show." Now I knew what Vi had meant when she said he talks "funnylike."

As they hurried off, giggling like three silly schoolgirls, he reentered the room, leaving the door slightly ajar. After a minute or two of hesitation, I took the liberty of stepping inside to find him seated with his back to me, busily engaged in sorting through a plethora of makeup jars on his dressing room table.

"Mr. Zambini?" I said, making him aware of my presence as I closed the door behind me. Startled, he looked up, catching my image in the mirror. "You forgot zomezing? Oh," he added, on turning halfway round to face me, "I thought you wair one of zee other ladies."

"I'm Mrs. Hudson," I said, adding a smile.

"Ah," he answered, returning the smile, "zee Great Zambini is always glad to see one of his many admirers. What can I do for you, madame?"

"To begin with, Mr. Zambini, you could start by dropping that silly accent of yours. Or, should I say, Mr. Oliver? Mr. Max Oliver, isn't it?" I added, grateful for having remembered the name from Mr. Wooley's account of him.

"Aye, it's Oliver!" he snapped after recovering himself from the initial shock of my disclosure. "What of it? There's plenty what knows my name."

"No doubt," I answered. "And speaking of names," I carried on, while doing my best to avert my gaze from those deep-pocketed eyes, "I've another I'm sure you're familiar with—Edgar Bramwell."

He had started to rise from his chair but on hearing the name fell back down into it. I was then the recipient of a most curious stare. "That woman— the other night—she was—she said—" His words were disjointed and for one brief moment I saw fear in his face. "Yes, I know the name—from reading

about him in the papers,'' was the gruff response as
he sought to regain his composure.

"I think not, Mr. Oliver. It's a little more involved
than that, I think.''

"Who are you?"

"I told you," I answered. "My name is Mrs.
Hudson. The other woman you spoke of is Mrs.
Warner, my associate. We're investigating the mur-
der of Edgar Bramwell.''

"You're not with the coppers?"

"They're aware of our investigation.''

"She spoke of Sherlock Holmes," he said, in reference to Violet, as if wishing me to elaborate further.

"Yes, that's right," I answered, hoping he'd let
it go at that. If the name Holmes carried more weight
with him than that of Hudson, so be it. The end
result was what mattered.

"He's involved in this as well, is he?" he pressed.

"Did you think he wouldn't be?" I replied, knowing that when one wants to sidestep the truth the best
course of action is to answer one question with another. He accepted my response with a doleful shake
of his head before turning his back to me to fish
around the bottom drawer of his table. "If you're
looking for a pendant to swing before my eyes, Mr.
Oliver," I spoke up on taking note of his rummaging, "you'd best forget it. That trick won't work
twice.''

"What? No, no, it's not that, it seems someone's
nicked my bottle of—'ere, how'd you know about
the pendant?''

I presented him with a smile the Cheshire cat
would have been proud of. He eyed me for the long-

est moment. "You're too smart by half, you are," he said at last. Did I detect a tinge of admiration in his voice?

"Now then, my dear sir," I announced, "let's get down to business, shall we? You *were* at the Bramwell residence on the night of the murder, weren't you?"

"You're trying to incriminate me, that's what you're trying to do," he answered in a most belligerent tone of voice. "I've got my rights. You're not the police."

"And it's a good thing for you I'm not, my man," I shot back. "As of now the police are unaware of your involvement. As to incrimination, you incriminated yourself the minute I found this in the very room the man was murdered in." I then very dramatically withdrew from my coat pocket the calling card he had presented to Vi. It was a bluff, but it worked.

"All right, curse you! I *was* there! But I didn't—I mean, it's not what you—" Three sharp raps from outside interrupted any further continuance.

"Five minutes, Mr. Zambini," sang out a youthful voice from beyond the door.

"Look," he pleaded, "we can't talk now. You heard—I'm on in five minutes. Tonight, my hotel, midnight. Here's the address," he added, taking his card from me and, in a most agitated fashion, scribbling down the information before handing it back.

"I couldn't possibly tonight," I told him, for I had no intention of meeting with him alone in his hotel room be it midnight or any other time of the day or night. Mr. Wooley, I thought, yes, I'd speak to him tomorrow. I was sure he'd come. "Tomorrow, Mr. Oliver,'' I stated, ''would best suit my needs and midnight then, if it suits yours. And I want answers, mind,'' I added. ''Remember, you can talk to me or, if not, you can talk to Scotland Yard.''

''Yes, yes,'' he agreed. ''I understand. Tomorrow, at midnight then, Mrs. Hudson.''

NINE

Case Solved?

~ "WELL, I HOPE you're not thinking of traipsing off to meet him in his hotel room tonight by yourself—and at midnight at that! Why, I never heard of such a thing." So spoke Violet the following morning as she stood framed within the bedroom door addressing me in what she considered righteous indignation while I calmly set about the making of our bed.

"I'm not so foolish as all that, m'girl. No," I added, smoothing out a pillow, "I thought I'd see if perhaps Mr. Wooley might be interested in, how shall I say, escorting me to my rendezvous with 'zee Great Zambini.' "

"Oh, Zambini's great all right," announced my companion in a show of disgust. "A great twit, if you asks me. But, 'ere," she carried on, "what's all this business about Mr. Wooley? There's no need to be asking him. What do you think I'm here for, eh?''

''You!'' I exclaimed, completely taken aback. ''I thought you said you had enough of him.''

''Aye, well, be that as it may, it'd be better than sitting here all night by myself wondering what if anything had happened to you.''

While I didn't anticipate coming to any physical harm, it's true one couldn't be too careful. A second party, be it Violet or Mr. Wooley, would certainly give our Mr. Zambini pause should he consider taking such action. And since Vi and I were getting to be old hands at this sort of thing, I readily agreed on her coming along, if, as I told her, she was really serious in wanting to accompany me.

''Well, 'course I am,'' she announced quite adamantly. ''We're a team, we are.''

''Then perhaps,'' I added with a sideways glance in her direction, ''you'd be good enough to give your old teammate a hand with this bed.''

''I'll never understand why you're so set on making it first thing in getting up,'' she grumbled good-naturedly on making her way round the other side. ''Just close the door, I say. Out of sight, out of mind.''

''I sometimes wish I could do just that with this investigation of ours. It's on my mind every waking hour.''

''Got any ideas as yet as to how it was done or who done it?''

''How it was done? An inkling, at best,'' I answered. But as to who actually planned it and carried it out—not as yet,'' I admitted.

''You don't think it was Zambini, then?''

''I'd say he was a party to it in some way. But

no, I don't think he did the actual shooting.''

''But like you were telling me last night, you did get him to admit he was there, right?''

''True—our first real break in the case. That puts us one up on the Yard,'' I added, affording myself a small but satisfied smile.

''One thing puzzles me though,'' spoke Vi with an appropriate puzzled look, ''if, as he says, he were there, like, then why didn't any of the others mention they saw him, eh?''

''That, my dear Mrs. Warner,'' I announced, ''is just one of the questions I intend to put to him.''

''You don't think he'll skip out on us, do you?''

''I doubt it very much. Remember, he still has the rest of his engagement at the theater to fulfill. Besides,'' I added with a smile, harking back in thought to the previous evening, ''I believe I was somewhat successful in putting the fear of not only Scotland Yard but of Sherlock Holmes into him. No,'' I mused, ''I think our Mr. Zambini will stay put all right.''

''Aye, and I'll be that surprised when we see him if he doesn't tell us it was that Mr. Moore as being the one behind it all.''

''Why do you say that?''

''Why? I'll tell you straight out, Emma Hudson— I never liked that man right from the start,'' she stated, as if that in itself explained everything.

''Oh, well, then,'' I chided her, ''that's reason enough, I'd say.''

''It's not just that,'' she carried on, taking my little aside at face value, ''it's what you were telling me last night about your meeting with him and all. I mean, all that falderal 'bout how life has treated him so badly. Badly, he says! Not so bad as some I've known and you too, like as not. It's all an act, you see. Trying to get your sympathy like, so you'll look elsewhere. Throw you off the track, so to speak. Aye, that's what I think. 'Ere, luv,'' she suddenly announced, breaking off her tirade, ''give us a hand in straightening out the counterpane, will you? It's hanging down too far on this side. There, that's got it,'' she said seemingly quite pleased with herself and adding somewhat condescendingly that I could now sit down to breakfast with a clear conscience— ''seeing as how the bed was made now, and all.''

''You've already eaten then, have you?'' I asked, ignoring her barbed comment.

''Aye, a nice hot bowl of oatmeal. But never you worry,'' she added reassuringly, ''I've made enough for you as well.''

I winced. It was not exactly my favorite morning dish. If there was one thing, no, make that two things, I could never quite forgive the Scots for it was oatmeal and the bagpipes. Fortunately, I had only one of the two to contend with this morning. ''By the way,'' I said, on stepping from bedroom to kitchen, ''I think you're wrong about Mr. Moore, I had the feeling—now who can that be?'' I asked, breaking off in mid-sentence on hearing a knocking at the front door.

''Probably some salesman getting an early start, like as not,'' she remarked. ''I'll see to it. You best eat your oatmeal 'fore it gets cold,'' she added, taking herself off down the hall.

As I began to ladle this less than epicurean delight into my bowl, I caught the sound of a male voice conversing with Vi at the door. I know that voice from somewhere, I thought, but where? Then I re-membered.

"It's Inspector MacDonald," announced Vi as she followed the gentleman into the kitchen. "Come to pay us a call, he has."

"Inspector," I said, smiling pleasantly enough while wondering what in the world it was that brought him to our door, "how nice to see you. Come in and sit yourself down."

"Good morning, Mrs. Hudson. Thank you, I will. I was just saying to Mrs. Warner," he added on taking his place at the table, "that I hope you both will forgive me for such an early call."

"Think nothing of it, Inspector. I just hope you'll forgive us for not looking our best at such an hour," I replied, while self-consciously adjusting the collar of my housecoat. "Actually, we're usually up long before this."

"Aye," added Vi, taking her place beside me, "we both slept in a little later this morning. 'Course, even at that, I was up before Em here," she added smugly.

"Och, don't be fretting yourselves about it, la-dies," he answered with a wave of his hand. "You should see my wee wifey in the morning. Aye, now, there's a sight for you."

"Looks worse than we do, does she?" chided Vi.

"Aye. No—I mean—ah, now, Mrs. Warner," he laughed, "I'm afraid you've boxed me into a corner on that one."

"Perhaps you'd care for a cup of tea, Inspector?"

"Tea, you say, Mrs. Hudson? That I would, ma'am. If it's no bother."

"No bother at all," I answered on rising.

"Would that be oatmeal you have there?" he asked, eyeing my bowl as I poured his tea, and knowing full well that it was.

"Indeed it is," I was quick to answer on seeing my chance. "Here, it's yours if you wish," I said on sitting myself down and edging it toward him, adding as a further inducement (though as I rightly suspected none was needed) that it was still piping hot.

"I'll not be one to take your breakfast from you, Mrs. Hudson," he answered with eyes that never left the bowl.

"Nonsense," said I, blithely brushing aside his less than persuasive pronouncement. "I'm not really all that hungry."

"Perhaps I will then," he said after but a moment's hesitation. "For I'll not be knowing of a better way to start off a day than with a good hot bowl of oatmeal under my belt."

I could think of a hundred but I let it pass. "Tell me, Inspector," I asked as he continued to spoon it up, all the while quite oblivious to the two who sat before him, "what is it that brings you here?"

"Perhaps," spoke Vi, with a wink in my direction, "his 'wee wifey' didn't give him his breakfast this morning."

"There's more truth than you think in what you say, Mrs. Warner. What with my irregular hours Mrs. MacDonald and I get very little chance to sit down at the table together. But you asked me the reason for my visit, Mrs. Hudson," he continued, giving one last lick to his spoon before resetting it back into the now empty bowl. "My reasons are twofold, ma'am. One, to apologize for being a bit sharp with you two ladies when first we met at the Bramwell residence. No, no," he carried on, seeing I was about to wave aside his apology as being unwarranted, "it's true. My only excuse being the strain I was under. I don't mind telling you my superiors had me up on the carpet that very day about the lack of progress in the case."

"We understand perfectly, Inspector," I answered. "And as for the second reason?"

"The second reason," he beamed, "is the good news I bring."

"Good news, you say?" interjected Vi. "Well, it took you a flippin' long time to get around to it."

"Savoring the moment, ma'am," he smiled. "Savoring the moment."

"Out with it then," she added, becoming more than a little impatient with the man. As indeed, was I. What, I wondered, could this "good news" of his be? Had he found out about Zambini's involvement in the murder? If so, that put us neck in neck with the Yard in regard to our own inquiry.

"The investigation into the murder of Edgar Bramwell," began the inspector as Vi and I leaned eagerly forward hanging on his every word, "is now officially closed."

Needless to say we were left completely stunned.

"Closed? I—I don't understand," I managed to blurt out, being more than a little bewildered by what I had just heard.

"It's simple enough," he replied, sitting back with a smug little smile while seeming to enjoy the look of consternation on the two faces opposite him. "We now know who it was that shot Edgar Bramwell. Therefore, the case, for all intents and purposes, ladies, is closed.''

'' 'Ere, don't keep us in suspense then! Who was it that done him in, eh?''

"Arthur Moore," he stated simply enough.

"Arthur Moore!" The name fell from my mouth.

"You see, Em," sang out Violet, her face flushed in triumph, "I told you as much, didn't I? Said it were him, I did, Inspector, not more than five minutes 'fore you arrived."

"Then I congratulate you, Mrs. Warner."

I couldn't believe my ears. How could I have been so wrong? I had mentally put Arthur Moore at the bottom of my list. Could Vi have been right that it had all been a ploy on his part? "And he's actually confessed, has he, Inspector?" I asked, still finding it hard to resign myself to what I had heard.

"There was no confession, Mrs. Hudson," he informed me. "The gentleman in question is dead. Hanged himself, ma'am."

This was too much! "But that's impossible, Inspector MacDonald, I spoke to him just last night. Surely there's been some mistake."

"There's no mistake, Mrs. Hudson. The man was found last night hanging by his neck from a chandelier in the home of—''

"Mrs. Hamilton," I answered for him. He nodded. It was true then. "And he was found by—?"

"Miss Armstrong-Jones, ma'am. At approximately ten o'clock last night. I believe it was the maid who summoned a constable on the lady's request, who in turn informed the Yard, who in turn woke me up out of my sleep and—well, you can take it from there."

"And Miss Armstrong-Jones," I asked, "how did she appear to be holding up?"

"Poorly, Mrs. Hudson, as you can imagine. It could not have been a pretty sight for her. Had to cut the man down myself when I got there. By the time I left, she had taken a sedative and retired to her bed."

"And who could blame her, eh?" chimed in Vi. "Imagine walking into a room, nice as you please, and finding your hubby-to-be swinging from a chandelier, like."

"Oh, Vi, please."

"What? What'd I say?"

"You could at least be a little more—oh, let it go," I answered with a resigned sigh.

"You mentioned that you met with the man last night, Mrs. Hudson," spoke the Inspector. "We know that, of course. Which, I suppose you could say, would be a third reason for my visit."

" 'Ere, now, you're not saying Em here had anything to do with it?"

"Good heavens, no, Mrs. Warner," he readily assured her. "It was, as I say, a suicide, pure and simple."

"Somehow, Inspector," I spoke up, "I never thought of suicide as being either pure or simple."

"Quite right, Mrs. Hudson," he acknowledged. "Quite right. A poor choice of words on my part. Now then," he carried on, idly toying with his spoon, "as to your meeting with him last night—he sent for you, did he?"

"No," I answered. "Actually I arrived unannounced at approximately eight o'clock and left shortly thereafter."

"And the purpose of your visit being—?"

"Simply a followup to my previous question and answer session with him."

"I see. And how would you describe his general demeanor?"

"I found him to be in a state of deep depression," I answered honestly enough.

He put the spoon down and smiled. Obviously it was the answer he was looking for. "That corresponds exactly with the account given by Miss Armstrong-Jones and the maid, Bessie Smith. I should say that pretty well wraps it up."

"Wraps it up!" exclaimed Vi. "How'd he do it then, with nobody seeing him and all, eh? That's what I'd like to know!"

"I was just about to ask the same thing," I added.

Inspector MacDonald looked decidedly uncomfortable. "As I mentioned earlier," he answered, after a nervous clearing of his throat, "the man made no oral confession to anyone nor was there a note of any kind left."

"Then what you're saying," I said, "is that you or, for that matter, Scotland Yard, have no idea how the murder was actually carried out."

"I'm afraid the gentleman has taken that secret with him to the grave, Mrs. Hudson."

Has he indeed, I thought. Somehow it all sounded a little too neat and tidy. I had visions of the top brass at the Yard huddled together happily congratulating themselves on their good fortune. Arthur Moore, one of the suspects, hangs himself. Ergo— Moore is now declared the murderer. Why? Being no longer able to live with his guilt, he took his own life. They have witnesses, myself included, who will testify to his being in a state of deep depression. As to the question of how the murder was carried out, the inspector will no doubt be quick to inform the press that in the absence of any note of explanation, it was a secret that only Arthur Moore himself would ever know. I just didn't believe it was all that simple. It seemed that what had been not only a frustrating but unsolvable crime was now to be swept under the judicial rug.

"Inspector," I spoke up, "I don't know quite how to say this but, notwithstanding the fact that, as you say, for all intents and purposes the case has now been solved, I believe there is something you should know. I have a meeting tonight with a man who has admitted to me that he was at the Bramwell residence on the night of the murder. And," I added, "I have reason to believe that in some way he played a part in it."

Inspector MacDonald did not look altogether pleased. "Who is this man?" he asked.

"The Great Zambini," answered Vi.

"Who?"

"Zambini's his stage name, Inspector," I informed him. "Actually his name is Oliver. Max Oliver. He's currently appearing at the Alhambra."

"Is he? I see."

It was hardly the reaction I had expected.

"While I'm sure you believe what you have told me is of some significance, Mrs. Hudson," he said, very nicely, mind you, "I wouldn't put too much stock, if any, in what he's told you." I didn't know quite how to respond. Noting my somewhat puzzled look, he informed me that as of yesterday the Yard has had a total of fourteen people who have come forward to "confess" to the crime. "You wouldn't believe the stories they tell us," he said. "Each one more bizarre than the next."

"Like what?" questioned Vi.

"I had one old duffer who wandered into the Yard not more than two days ago," he answered with a light chuckle, obviously relishing the retelling of the tale. "I've come to give meself up, he says. It were me that killed that Mr. Brantwell—didn't even get the name right, you see. And how, I asked him, did you do it with no one seeing you? Wrapped meself up in an invisible cloak, he tells us. And quite serious he was, too. How, Sergeant Formby asks him, did you find the cloak to put it on, if it was invisible? The old boy was still trying to think of an answer to that one while we very politely ushered him out the door."

Any other time I might have seen the humor in it but not at that particular moment. "Inspector Mac-Donald," I stated, "I can well imagine you've had your share of cranks, but I assure you—"

"I know, I know," he quickly responded, cutting me off in mid-sentence, "you believe this Zam— Zam?" He turned to Vi.

"—bini," she said.

"Yes, you believe this Zambini chappie is quite serious in what he says, we've had those too," he added in an aside, "but what they all seek is a form of perverse publicity for themselves. Now, you say, this person is an entertainer of some sort. Well, ma'am, I ask you, you know how showfolk are— write anything you want as long as you spell my name right, isn't that what they say? Of course," he continued, "you're free to see him or anyone else if you've a mind to. I only offer you my advice for what it's worth.''

While responding by thanking him for his good intentions on my behalf, I had a sudden inspiration. ''Inspector MacDonald,'' I said, ''you have, as you stated, your murderer, albeit, I'm sorry to say, a dead one. However, what you don't have is the answer as to how the crime was committed. Crank confessions aside, I have my reasons for believing Zambini played a major role in the murder. Now, would it not present a more tidy package to the press and public alike if you could supply them with the details as to how it was carried out?''

He eyed me warily. ''Just what are you getting at, Mrs. Hudson?''

''Hold off announcing the news of Moore's suicide to the papers for two days and,'' I added with all the confidence I could muster, ''I'll give you the answer.''

''Two days!'' he exclaimed. ''Why you must be daft, woman. I couldn't keep it from the press for two days even if I wanted to. And what are you hanging this upcoming revelation of yours on—this Zambini chap of yours? A slender thread at best, Mrs. Hudson.''

''A thread, nonetheless, Inspector.''

He answered with a disapproving shake of his head. ''Two days? I just don't see how I—''

''One, then,'' I bargained.

He studied me in silence for a moment or two, no doubt giving thought to the realization that if indeed I could pull it off, it would be quite a feather in his cap. A very large feather indeed for, as the officer in charge of the investigation, it would be his responsibility to report his findings to both his superiors and the press, with the end result very well being a move up in rank to the position of chief inspector. And should I fail, what had he to lose? "You're sure Moore and Zambini were in on this together, are you?" he asked.

"I'm sure that our Mr. Zambini played a part in it, yes," I answered, neatly sidestepping round his question. I was still not convinced that Arthur Moore has been his partner in crime and thought it best not to debate the point at that particular moment in time.

"Twenty-fours it is, then, Mrs. Hudson."

I breathed a sigh of relief, thanked him, and hoped to high heaven I could live up to my part of the bargain.

"Mr. Holmes wouldn't be up and about by any chance, would he?" queried the inspector as Vi and I escorted him down the hall.

"I shouldn't think so," answered Violet. "Should have heard him by now if he were. Though he should be down 'fore too long for a bite of something. Eats like a bird, he does. Why'd you ask?"

"Oh, it's just that I would have liked to let him know about my solving—that is to say, about the Yard solving the mystery of who shot Edgar Bramwell," he answered as if it were no more than an afterthought.

Now isn't that interesting, I thought, realizing his answer was not so casual a one as he would have us imagine. It led me to speculate whether his visit had been not only to inform both Violet and myself as to what he believed was the conclusion of the case but, hopefully, that his news might win him the plaudits of Sherlock Holmes himself. If that were so, Mr.

Holmes's absence might just have saved the inspector from a future embarrassment if, and I emphasize the word "if," I was fortunate enough to prove the real murderer was still out there. In any event, Vi and I politely bid him a good day at the door but not before I had assured him I would certainly relay his news to Mr. Holmes.

"Then a good morning to you, Mrs. Hudson, Mrs. Warner," he acknowledged with a tip of his hat. "Remember," he added on stepping out into the street, "twenty-four hours."

No sooner had Vi closed the door than she whirled on me. "Twenty-four hours!" she exclaimed. "What's all this business about twenty-four hours—twenty-four years would be more like it."

"What choice did I have?" I answered back with a resigned sigh. "Think about it, Vi. As soon as the inspector makes an official announcement that Arthur Moore is the murderer of Edgar Bramwell, our suspects are free to fly the coop, as it were. And then where would we be? Remember, the MacPhails have already been seen checking out passage fares."

"Let 'em sail to China, for all I care," she answered indifferently. "Suspects, she says. What suspects? I'd like to know. You heard what the inspector said about Mr. Moore being the one who done it. I thought you wanted time to find out *how* it were done."

"That, too," I said. "As for Mr. Moore, he's no more guilty than you are. I'm sure of it. The man was depressed, I'll grant you that. But I was never left with the feeling," I added by way of explanation, "it was because he had taken a life. Rather, it was because he believed the life he had known had been taken from him.'' By the look on Vi's face, I could see she was not entirely convinced. Obviously she felt that if both she and the inspector agreed on Mr. Moore's guilt, that should be good enough for me as well. ''All I can say,'' she stated, ''is you've got to prove it to me, you have, Emma Hudson.''

''And a few others as well, I should imagine,'' I muttered to myself as we made our way back down to the kitchen.

''Sounds like he's up,'' said Vi, pausing in her step as we passed the staircase.

''Perhaps it's the doctor,'' I offered up.

''No,'' she said, as we entered the kitchen, ''he were up when I was. He's already left for some such appointment or other. Might's well fix up some oatmeal for his nibs—do him good, I say. And for you as well,'' she added, ''seeing as how the inspector gobbled down your helping.''

Knowing Mr. Holmes's aversion to the cereal was equalled only by my own, I wondered what his reaction would be when the bowl was set before him. As for myself, I managed a weak smile.

''Still seeing Zambini tonight, are we?'' she asked, rummaging through the cupboard.

''We are indeed, Mrs. Warner,'' I replied. ''We are indeed.''

TEN

The Final Curtain

"DING IT AGAIN, Em."

I did as she advised by once more bringing my hand down three times quite sharply on the little desk bell to the front of us. It may not have been loud enough to raise the dead but it did have the desired effect of waking a decidedly rotund desk clerk who had been sitting wedged within his chair with head drooped to chest in a state of deep slumber. As his eyes slowly fluttered open, chubby little hands commenced to rub sleep from them. Focusing in on us and forgoing the effort required of him to rise from his chair, he stated, quite rudely I thought, that we could have left our hotel key on the counter without the need of disturbing him.

"Aye, we could have if we were staying here," stated my companion. "But it's Mr. Zambini we've come to see."

"What! Calling on guests at this hour?" he exclaimed. "Why, it's near midnight, it is."

"Think we're a couple of tarts, do you?" was Violet's abrasive rejoinder.

"Oh, Vi, really!" I said, turning on her with a most annoyed look.

In turn, we two elderly ladies were slowly scrutinized up and down by the hotel clerk. "Tarts?" he repeated, bringing his hand up to his mouth to cover a smile. "Hardly."

Ignoring him, I pressed on. "We have a business appointment with Mr. Zambini," I explained. "But I'm afraid I've forgotten his room number. It's either 323 or 332. Perhaps, if you could check and see—?"

He struggled out of his chair, scowling all the while to show his displeasure at our having disturbed him and, once at the counter, flipped open the hotel guest book. "There's no Zambini here," he growled, after running a fat forefinger down the list of registered names.

"He's pulled a fast one on us, he has," whispered Vi. "Knew he would."

"I can't believe he—oh, wait a minute," I said, turning my attention back to the night clerk. "Try Oliver. Max Oliver."

I was the recipient of a most suspicious stare from two piggy little eyes. "What's your game, missus?" he demanded to know. "First you say you want to see a Mr. Zam—something or other. Now it's this here—"

"Oliver," I haughtily informed him on repeating the name while trying my best not to look altogether foolish. "Max Oliver. Zambini is his stage name."

"Showfolk," he muttered. "Should have known. Here it is," he said, after another rundown of the names. "Max Oliver. He's in Room 323. There's a lift over there to your right," he added on returning to the comfort of his chair.

We entered the lift, ascended to the third floor, and stepped out.

"Not exactly the Ritz," commented Vi as we made our way down a well-aged hallway of worn carpet.

"I've seen worse," I answered. The hotel, while not a fashionable one, was what one might call respectable at best. "Ah, here it is," I said, on arriving at the designated door. I rapped lightly and waited. No answer. Vi and I exchanged questioning glances and, believing I had heard a sound from within, I pressed my ear to the door.

"Hear anything?" she asked.

I answered no with a shake of my head. "For a moment there," I said, "I thought I—" I knocked again, a little more forcefully this time. Still no answer.

" 'Ere," questioned my companion, "you sure you've got the right room?"

"Yes, I think so. He did say 323, didn't he?"

"Aye, that's what he told us. Looks like all this has been for nowt, if you ask me," she added in some annoyance as we continued to wait for a response from within.

I knocked again. "Mr. Oliver, are you there?" I called out. "It's Mrs. Hudson."

"Face it, Em," advised Violet, "he's skipped out on us, he has."

"Wait a minute. Listen," I said. "I heard something. There it is again. It sounded like a man's voice—muffled. Did you hear it?''

"Your hearing's better than mine," she admitted, pressing her ear to the door. "I can't hear a ruddy thing."

"There's someone in there, I'm sure of it," I said, becoming more than a little annoyed myself.

"Well, we can't stand out here in the hallway all night," she stated. "I'm all for high-tailing it home. How 'bout you?"

In lieu of an answer I reached for the doorknob and gave it a twist. The door was unlocked! I turned to my companion with a questioning look, wondering to myself whether or not to enter. "Might's well," said Vi, as if reading my mind.

I called out his name as we hesitantly stepped inside. I received no reply. On the wall, a flickering, yellowish glow from a single, solitary gas lamp cast the room into a myriad of nightmarish shadows, made all the worse, from what we could make out, by the figure of a man sprawled face down halfway across the bed. The sight was enough to stop us in our tracks and, with eyes becoming more accustomed to what little light that was afforded us, I could make out bedsheets in disarray, a pillow cast to one side of the room, and an overturned chair. I sprang to the bed with Vi close behind.

"Look!" she exclaimed, with eyes riveted in horror to one particular spot on the bed. I turned my gaze to the area in question and saw what appeared to be a good-sized carving knife lying half-hidden beneath the folds, its blade of wet crimson contrasting most vividly with sheets of white linen. "He's been stabbed!" she cried out, quite visibly shaken in body and voice. "That's what happened to him—he's been stabbed!"

"For heaven's sake, woman," I responded quite sharply, "get a hold of yourself! He needs our help, not your hysterics." And though I had been quick to rebuke her, in truth, I could hardly blame her for reacting as she had, for it was indeed a most horrific sight that presented itself before us.

"Still alive then, is he?" she asked, casting a wary eye at the inert body on the bed.

I bent over and, taking hold of his shoulder, managed to turn him round face up. "Just barely," I answered on viewing with sickening dismay the slow rhythmic heaving of the bloody-shirted chest. "Here, give me a hand," I said as I removed my scarf.

"To do what?"

"Help me raise him up a bit," I answered.

Lifting him as gently as we could, I slid my scarf under his back and around his chest, tightening and tying it as best as I was able. "That should stop the flow of blood," I announced. "At least to a certain extent. But, I'm afraid—Mr. Oliver," I called out softly on bending over that face of ashen gray. "Can you hear me?"

As his eyes slowly flickered open I received a faint smile of recognition. "Mrs. Hudson," he uttered up in a hoarse whisper, "I heard you at the door. I couldn't—"

"Yes, yes," I answered, brushing aside the unneeded apology, "no need to worry 'bout that now. What I *am* worried about," I added, "is that wound of yours. It looks very bad indeed." In truth, the man had the look of death about him.

"There's a bit of brandy still left in this bottle here," announced Vi, holding up her find for inspection. "Perhaps we should give him a sip or two."

"Yes, that might—No," I said, "on second thought, I'm not sure whether we should or not."

"A doctor," spoke the man, forcing out the words as he tried to raise himself up. "Perhaps in the hotel—?"

"Now you just lie back there, my good man," stated Vi. "You're in no condition to be moving about like that."

The deep-pocketed eyes turned slowly in the direction of my companion. "I know you," he said at last. "You're the woman—that night—my dressing room."

"Aye, that's right," she acknowledged. "But there's no need to go into that now."

His face exhibited a sudden spasm of pain. "Please," he moaned. "A doctor."

I looked at Vi. She nodded in silent agreement. It was evident to the two of us he had but minutes to live. Knowing what had to be said and wishing it were someone other than myself who had to say it, I nevertheless screwed up my courage to inform the man it was too late to call for the assistance of a physician. The wound, I added, was fatal. Strangely enough, when I had concluded he seemed to rally. It was as if some small lingering spark of life, in defiance of the inevitability of its fate, refused to be extinguished so quickly.

"Dying, you say? Nonsense, madame," he answered between bouts of coughing. "Zee gods would never permit zee Great Zambini to take leave of life in such a dismal surrounding as this.''

Was the accented voice for effect or was he drift-
ing in and out of personalities? I had no idea. I only
knew that with his refusal to accept the truth of his
imminent demise, precious minutes were being lost.

"Please, Mr. Oliver," I begged, "you must believe me. You've not much time left. Tell me, who
was it that did this to you?"

"Obviously, a critic," he answered with a hollow
laugh, the effect of it forcing him to spit blood. It
was only then did he realize the gravity of his situation. "It's true then," he said, managing a weak
smile. "The play of life is over. The curtain de-
scends.''

"I'm afraid so," I answered.

"Ask what you will then," he responded, coughing out the words.

I wasted no time. "What part did you play in the
murder of Edgar Bramwell?" I asked.

"Went to perform there," he answered with no
little effort. "Told what to do—what to say. Didn't
know—didn't know."

"Didn't know what?" I asked. "That there was
a murder plot afoot?"

He answered yes, with a slight nodding of his
head.

"So you went there and did what was asked of
you."

"Mmmm."

"And Bramwell was still alive when you left?"

"Yes. Read about murder—next day—newspapers." The voice was weak. The breathing labored.
"He came—day after—gave me more money."

"And this same man who gave you additional

money to keep your silence is the same man who plunged a knife into you tonight. Is that right?''

"Yes—same," he managed to gasp out, adding, "so tired. So very tired."

"And this man," I pressed on at a hurrying pace, "who *is* he?"

My answer was no more than an odd little sound that emerged from the back of his throat as the head fell lifelessly forward onto his chest. I would learn no more from the late Great Zambini.

"Is he—?" asked Vi.

"He's gone," I answered.

"I think we best be as well," she said.

"We'll have to inform the police in any event," I added. "We can't just leave him lying there. Hello, what's this?"

"What?"

"This small piece of broken glass on the edge of the bed," I answered, picking it up and giving it close examination. "It appears to be the type of glass one finds in spectacles. Note the curvature and beveled edge," I added, handing it over to my companion for her inspection.

"Broken during the struggle, like as not," she said. "That'd be my guess."

"I agree—Max Oliver didn't wear glasses, did he?"

"Don't think so. But then you never know. He could have, in private, like."

"For this piece of glass to be found on the bed," I announced, "he would have to have been wearing them during the fight with his assailant."

"Aye, true enough," she agreed, handing back the fragmented glass.

"And yet," I mused, "there's something odd about this glass."

"Like what?"

"I don't know, really. In any event," I added, "let's find out if he did wear spectacles or not, shall we?"

" 'Ere, now!" she exclaimed as I bent over the body. "You're not going to go hunting through the bedsheets for them with him still lying there and all, are you?"

"There's no need to," I announced on returning to a standing position. "Max Oliver did not wear glasses."

"How'd you know that, then?"

"There are no indentations in the skin on either side of his nose that one would find if the man had been wearing spectacles," I informed my companion. "This," I stated, before dropping the glass into my purse, "belonged to the killer. A killer," I added, "that we missed just by minutes."

"Aye, and lucky for us we did. If we hadn't got into a mix-up of names and room numbers with Rip Van Winkle down there at the desk we could have been lying here dead like, as well. But how did he get away without us seeing him? Unless," she continued, in answer to her own question, "he were high-tailing it down the stairs as we were coming up in the lift."

"Possibly. Although," I added, walking over to the half-open window within the room, "I believe this would have been a quicker and less inconspicuous way than charging down a flight of steps."

"But we're on the third floor," she argued.

"Complete with fire escape," I informed her, tak-

ing in the metal stairs leading down into the darkness
below. As I continued my stance at the window, it
seemed as if all London lay fast asleep. For, with
the exception of a passing motor car, the shadows
of night had blanketed the city in an eerie silence.
As I turned from the window, a thought suddenly
occurred to me.

"What?" asked Vi.

"What?" I repeated. "What do you mean,
what?"

"You've got a funny look on your face," she
said.

"Thank you very much, I'm sure," I answered.

"You know what I mean. It's that look you have
when you get one of them funny ideas."

"Well," I answered, "I don't know how funny it
is, but it is an idea."

"Let's hear it then."

"Later," I said, "when we've more time. "As for
now, I think we best be off."

"What about the knife?" she asked. "Should we
examine it?"

"No need. Leave it for Scotland Yard," I advised.
"We don't want to be accused of tampering with
evidence."

"Like that broken piece of glass?" she smiled.
"Saw you put in your purse, I did."

"Right now," I answered, closing the door behind
us, "it's more important to me than to the police."

"Heading home, are we?" she asked as we de-
scended down in the lift.

"By rights, we should take ourselves over to the
nearest police station. Although," I added, "there's
one place I had hoped to—Ah, it appears we've at

least been saved a trip to the constabulary," I announced as we stepped out into the lobby. For standing there, as nice as you please, was a police officer enjoying a cup of tea with the night clerk.

"Constable," I was quick to inform him on our approach, "something terrible has happened. The man in Room 323 has been murdered. We were to meet him there tonight, you see, and when we arrived—"

"What's this!" exclaimed the officer. "A man, murdered, you say?"

"Aye, that's right," contributed Vi. "Stabbed to death, he was."

"Showfolk," groaned the hotel desk clerk. "Knew there'd be trouble, I did."

"You two best come along with me," stated the constable, hastily setting down his cup. "We'll have ourselves a look-see, shall we? Room 323, was it?" he asked on ushering us over to the lift.

"Yes, that's right," I replied. "But if you don't mind, my friend and I would rather take the stairs. I'm afraid the lift has left us both with queasy stomachs."

"I know what you mean," he sympathized. "My missus has the same problem with them. Mr. Dibley," he called out, addressing the hotel clerk, "I'll want you to come along with me as well. We'll meet you ladies upstairs then," he added in an aside to the two of us. For his part, Mr. Dibley wedged his body out of his chair and, mumbling away to himself, waddled over to where the constable stood waiting.

As Vi and I started off toward a door marked "stairs," the two men entered the lift. No sooner had they begun their ascent than I placed my hand on Vi's arm in a gesture of restraint. "This is as far as we go," I announced.

"Eh? I thought we were going—"

"We don't have the time," I answered. "Heaven only knows how long we'll be with the constable. And if he should decide to take us to the station for further questioning—well, you see what I mean."

"So that's what all that business was about with our having queasy stomachs and all," she grinned. "You wanted the constable to take the lift so we could hop it. Always thinking, you are, Emma Hudson. But, I mean," she added on a serious note, "we could get in trouble, we could, leaving the scene of a murder, as they say."

"Not to worry," I assured her. "Well do our explaining to Inspector MacDonald tomorrow."

"But today's tomorrow."

"Oh, lord, you're right," I groaned as we turned on our heels and headed across the lobby to the open street. "We now have less than twenty-four hours to come up with a solution."

Once outside we thought ourselves quite fortunate in spotting and hailing down a cab. However, on reigning up the cabbie informed us that due to the lateness of the hour he'd be taking no more fares and indeed was most anxious to get along home himself. It was only after I had assured him that a goodly tip was in the offing did he consent to deliver us to our destination.

"Where to, then?" he asked once we had stepped inside and settled down.

I gave him the address of the Bramwell residence.

"We're not going there now, are we!" exclaimed

Violet. "At this time of night? Why, they'll all be in bed, they will."

"I certainly hope so," I answered with a smile.

Poor Violet was thoroughly confused and, I'll admit, a trifle annoyed.

"All right, Emma Hudson," said she, "out with it. What's this all about then, eh?"

"That piece of glass we found tonight," I said. "It set me to wondering."

"About what?"

"About who I knew that wore glasses."

"Oh, well, that's easy," she replied. "First off, you and I do, on occasion. Then there's that Mrs. Gormley from across the street—"

"Oh, Vi," I groaned, "I mean, who among our suspects."

"Didn't say that, did you?" she retorted. "Right, then. If you're talking suspects, Mr. Moore does, or did," she added, correcting herself. "But it wouldn't be his what with him being dead and all. No one else that I can think of."

"Mrs. Birdie does," I said.

"What! You mean the child's governess? You think she—?"

"No, it was just a thought I had at the time. Although she is a big, heavyset woman who would have the weight to grapple with a man. No, as I say, it was a thought I quickly discounted when I realized that there was something odd about that piece of glass. Here," I said, removing it from my purse, "take a look through it."

She held it up to her eye, squinted and, on handing it back, announced she saw nothing out of the ordinary.

"Exactly," I smiled. "If this had been part of an eyeglass made to a prescription, your vision would have been distorted. As indeed, it would for anyone who wears spectacles. What you were looking through, my dear Mrs. Warner," I stated, carefully replacing it back in my purse, "was clear glass."

"Clear glass?" was the bewildering response. "Then, if it's not from a pair of spectacles, what, then?"

"Goggles," I answered.

"Goggles?" she questioned. "What kind of goggles? Oh," she said, her face lighting up in the realization of the answer, "you mean the kind them drivers wear when they—. The Bramwell car!" she exclaimed. "So that's why we're going there—to check out the car, right?"

"I would have liked to have left it till tomorrow," I answered. "But, as you so succinctly put it, today's tomorrow, and we're desperately running out of time."

"But what," she asked, "made you think of goggles in the first place?"

"It's strange how things happen," I answered. "As I was looking out the hotel window, I caught a glimpse of a motor car passing by below. It was then I realized what had puzzled me about that piece of glass. It was clear. Not spectacles, I thought, but goggles. From there it was just a mental hop, skip, and a jump from—"

"—the goggles to the automobile to the Bramwell car what that Mr. Burke always seems to be doodlin' around in, right?"

"Something like that," I answered. "And speaking of the Bramwells," I added, clutching the handstrap for safety's sake as our carriage careened round a corner at a galloping pace, "I just hope we arrive there all in one piece. No doubt our driver is in a hurry to drop us off and be on his way home."

"More'n likely he's in a bigger hurry to collect his tip," was my companion's wry comment.

"You could be right," I laughed.

"One thing about this case puzzles me though," announced Vi as we continued to proceed ever onward through the empty streets of night.

"Only *one* thing? I wish I could say the same," I answered, for which I received a playful nudge to my side.

"You know what I mean," she said. "Thing is, I keep thinking 'bout Mr. Moore and all," she went on. "If the inspector believes he was the murderer—"

"Which he wasn't," I interjected.

"Aye, I suppose you're right there," she grudgingly admitted. "But what I mean is, why did someone bother to kill Zambini? The case was closed as far as Scotland Yard was concerned. The real murderer should have left well enough alone, if you ask me. All this does," she added with a perplexing shake of her head, "is open up another kettle of fish."

"Look at it this way," I said. "Arthur Moore commits suicide. Scotland Yard, under pressure to find a solution to the case, seizes on his suicide by announcing Moore as the murderer of Edgar Bramwell. But there are three people, aside from ourselves, who know that to be untrue. The murderer, his accomplice, and, until his death, Zambini. But what to do with Zambini? That was their problem.

For all they knew he could decide somewhere along the way to demand more and more money for his silence or eventually snap under the pressure of what he knew and confess all to the police. The man, as we ourselves knew, could be highly erratic at times. From their point of view it would be best to get rid of him.''

"I see," said Vi, nodding her head very thoughtfully. "But Zambini said summat 'bout being paid off the night after the murder—why not the same night?"

"No doubt," I answered, "he would have received his fee for his act that night but, when the murder hit the front pages of the newspapers, our murderer realized Zambini would put two and two together. Later, as I say, Zambini may have had second thoughts about either upping the ante or going to the police with his story. They make arrangements to meet in his hotel room to discuss the matter but, our Mr. X, having brought a knife along with him, knows only too well what the outcome of that meeting will be. With Zambini now out of the picture, no doubt our pair felt quite confident they have committed not only the perfect murder, but a most baffling one as well.''

"Aye, but little do they know," beamed Vi, "that we're hot on their trail. That's what the Yanks would say, hot on their trail.''

"Well, I have to admit the trail *is* getting a little warmer.''

"So," she said, rubbing her hands in glee, "all we have to do now is find out who did it and how it was done. Right?''

"Right.''

"But," she added after a momentary pause, "doesn't that put us right back where we started?"

"Oh, Vi," I cried out in exasperation. "Surely you'll admit we're further ahead now in what we know than when we started. It all takes time. We just have to keep adding little building blocks of information until we've completed the whole house, so to speak."

"The whole house, she says," muttered my companion. "Aye, just as long as it doesn't turn out to be a house of cards."

I made a face. "And you say *I'm* pessimistic? Cabbie," I called out with a tap to the roof, "this is far enough. I'd rather we didn't pull up right in front," I informed Vi, anticipating her question, "on the off chance someone in the household may still be up."

As we alighted from the hansom, I informed the cabbie to wait for us, adding that we'd be no more than fifteen minutes at best. He argued that he'd already put in a twelve-hour day and that both he and Mary needed their rest. Since the only two females present were Vi and myself, I concluded that the "Mary" he spoke of was his horse. When I put it to him that we would up the ante on his forthcoming tip, he readily agreed but not before first consulting with his horse. "What do you say, old girl?" he asked the mare. "Should we wait?" For her part, she answered, if that's the right word for it, by shaking that chestnut brown head of hers in an up and down motion and adding a soft little neighing sound into the bargain. "We stay," smiled the cabbie.

Having concluded our pact between both man and horse (this was indeed turning out to be a strange night), we set off down the street and, coming up to the Bramwells, Vi made mention of the fact that the motor car was nowhere to be seen. "I would imagine," I said, "they'd have it parked in the carriage house at back. This way," I added, indicating a narrow walkway between the Bramwell home and its counterpart on the other side which we then followed until at last coming round to the back of the residence where the carriage house stood.

"However will we get inside?" asked Vi.

"Look there," I answered, thankful for the light of a full moon. "That side door appears to be slightly ajar." On making our way over and finding that indeed it was, we entered and gazed in silent awe upon that great metal monster that stood before us like some regal beast, serene and secure within the confines of its den. "That shaft of moonlight helps," I said as we advanced ever closer. "But it would be better if—ah, there, see, a candle, on the shelf to your right."

"Where? Oh, aye, I see it," she acknowledged.

"Here, I may have a match," I said on rummaging through my purse.

"No need, luv," she answered. "There's a box full of 'em right next to it."

Before a light could be struck, an ungodly crash coming from somewhere over by the far wall split the air. What it was was unimportant—a tin of nails from the sound of it. What was important was that it left us transfixed with terror in the knowledge that we were not alone. We stood still as statues, hearing nothing but the beating of our hearts.

"You best come out," I said, addressing the unseen presence in a voice I hoped wouldn't betray my fears. A soft thud was heard atop the car. "I have a gun," I added, which in retrospect was a silly thing to say. For what if he had stepped out of the shadows to find I carried nothing more menacing than my purse? Thankfully, I wasn't put into the position of finding out.

"There's our mystery man for you," chortled Vi, pointing to the roof of the car.

I turned to see two unblinking eyes of yellow gazing down on us in feline curiosity. Having satisfied himself that his two human intruders were of no consequence, he took off as quickly and as silently as he had appeared.

"Nothin' but a flippin' cat," announced my companion. "Near gave me a heart attack, it did," she added, lighting the candle with a shaking hand.

As for myself, I heaved a heavy sigh of relief. "One needs to be strong of heart in this business," I said.

"Or daft," she added.

"At least we can be thankful it was nothing more than a cat," I remarked. I rested my hand on the automobile and, on doing so, uttered up a one-word comment. "Interesting."

"What is?" asked Vi.

"Put your hand here," I said, "on the car's bonnet."

"Whatever for?" was the apprehensive reply.

"Go ahead," I urged, seeing she was not all that keen on the idea. "It won't bite you," I added with a smile as she edged forward and gingerly placed the palm of her hand on the bonnet. "Doesn't it feel warm to you?" I asked.

"Aye, I suppose it does." She withdrew her hand. "Is that supposed to mean summat?"

"From what I understand," I answered, "when the motor has been running for a length of time, the heat it generates can be felt on the bonnet. The fact that it's still warm tells me the car has been recently driven."

"Think it's the same one you saw from the hotel window, do you?"

"It's possible. Let's have a look inside, shall we? Here, bring the candle closer, would you?" I asked on opening the car door. As she did, I could see a driver's duster strewn across the front seat. I removed it and dug my hand into the pockets. It was my guess our murderer had placed the driver's goggles in one of the pockets on his arrival at Zambini's hotel room and had broken them in a fall during their struggle. "Look!" I announced triumphantly on bringing forth my find. "Goggles."

"And cracked they are, too!" exclaimed Vi. "They must be—"

"They are, indeed," I answered. "See," I said, withdrawing the broken piece of glass from my purse and holding it up to the missing segment on the lens. "It fits perfectly." My companion congratulated me most heartily. I then replaced the goggles back in the pocket and the coat back on the front seat in more or less the same manner as I had found it, closed the car door, dropped the glass back into my purse, and announced it was now time we took our leave. "I shouldn't be too surprised," I said on closing the side door behind us, "if the murder weapon was found to be somewhere within the car as well."

"Shouldn't we go back inside and look for it?" she asked.

"There's no time," I answered. "We best be off. We've been fortunate that no one heard the crash or came to investigate it. We don't want to press our luck."

"I think we just have," she answered.

"Why, what do you mean?"

"Up there," she replied with eyes fixed on an upper-level window. "The light just went on. Look," she gasped, "there's someone behind the curtain!"

We froze in our tracks and remained as motionless as two old tree trunks. "If the moon suddenly decides to come out from behind those clouds," I whispered, "we're certain to be seen." I received no reply from Violet, who remained where she stood with eyes clenched tightly shut. Whether she believed this would help her in not being seen by someone else, I have no idea.

"What's happening now?" asked my unseeing friend.

"Nothing," I answered. "He's just standing there." I said "he" for I believed it to be a man from what I could see of that shadowy figure behind the curtain. "No, wait," I said, "he's moving away—the lights have gone off. It was probably someone who couldn't get to sleep." I added as we hastily made our way back between the houses and onto the street.

"Couldn't get to sleep, she says," grumbled Vi. "Well, *I* could, and no mistake! Why, it must be near three in the morning."

"I wonder what our cabbie will say," I said.

"I wonder what his horse will say," she added.

ELEVEN

Off We Go

AT APPROXIMATELY TWO o'clock the following afternoon, I hurried up the hall in response to a knocking at the front door and, on opening it, was greeted, if that's the right word for it, by a grim-faced Inspector MacDonald. "Inspector," I said, taking his coat and hat and ushering him into the parlor, "you've come somewhat early, haven't you? I believe I still have a few hours left of the twenty-four we agreed upon. But, here, take a seat by the fire and I'll fix us a nice cup of tea, if you like."

"A tea? I think not, Mrs. Hudson. I'm afraid my visit here today is not a social one," he added cordially enough but nonetheless officiously as he took his place beside the hearth. "And, as for our twenty-four-hour agreement, as you put it, whether that is still in effect will depend entirely on yourself."

"Myself?"

"There are a few questions I should like to have answered."

"My dear Inspector," I lightly replied, setting myself down on the sofa, "you needn't look so stern. I shall be glad to answer any and all questions that I can in regard to the Bramwell murder."

"The Bramwell—? My visit does not concern the Bramwell murder, Mrs. Hudson. In any event," he added in some annoyance, "I believe you were informed that case is closed. What I *would* like to know," he carried on, "is where you and Mrs. Warner were in the early hours of this morning—say, between midnight and one o'clock."

"Ah," I smiled, "so that's what this is all about. As a matter of fact," I answered truthfully, "I was just getting ready to take myself down to see you about that very matter when you arrived."

"Were you, indeed," was his dry response. I don't think he believed a word of it. "And your answer as to where you were then, would be—?"

"The Waverly Hotel," I answered. "We, Mrs. Warner and I, went there to see Max Oliver. But I believe you already knew that, didn't you, Inspector?"

"Aye, I did," he grudgingly admitted. "What with Constable Higgins's report of his description of the two women he had spoken to in the lobby plus the fact you had previously mentioned to me your intent on seeing this Oliver/Zambini person it was fairly obvious just who our two mystery women were. But," he added in all seriousness, "to skip out on the constable the way you did and, in doing so, leaving the scene of a murder, doesn't look good, Mrs. Hudson. Not good, indeed."

"Good heavens, Inspector," I answered with a laugh in the hope of enhancing the absurdity of the question, "surely you don't suspect me or Mrs. Warner of having anything to do with the man's death?"

"I'm not here as judge and jury, Mrs. Hudson, only to ask questions. By the by, where *is* Mrs. Warner?"

"Out doing an errand for me," I answered. "She should be back shortly." I was feeling decidedly uncomfortable about all this and wished to high heaven I had taken the time to accompany the constable. It was an error on my part and one I hoped wouldn't result in being denied the inspector's support and assistance that I would be in need of later.

"Now then," said he, breaking in on my thoughts, "let's start at the beginning, shall we? You say Mrs. Warner and yourself arrived at the hotel, went up to his room—and?"

"Went in," I answered.

"I see. The door was open, was it?"

"No, not open," I stated. "Unlocked. I knocked a few times and on receiving no answer, tried the door, found it was unlocked, and entered."

"And on entering you found the body of the murdered man sprawled on the bed. Is that correct?"

"Yes."

"And the knife?"

"On the bed as well. But," I added, "Zambini was still alive. Though just barely, mind you."

"Was he indeed? And yet," remarked the inspector glancing over his notes, "I have it down here, that according to the constable's report it was the shorter woman of the two who informed him, to quote her words, 'He's been stabbed to death.' That would be Mrs. Warner, would it not? I say that from observing on my previous visit here that you stand— what, a good inch and a half taller than she?''

"About that, I should say," I answered. "But," I added, "as to Mrs. Warner, she was quite correct in saying what she did. When we entered the room we saw that he'd been stabbed. When we exited the room he had, by then, expired. So, for all intents and purposes, he had been stabbed to death just as Mrs. Warner had so stated.''

"Mrs. Hudson," smiled the inspector for the first time since his arrival, "you're not in a court of law.''

"Not yet, at any rate," I answered, managing a smile in return.

"You say he wasn't dead when you entered," he continued. "Was his condition as such that he was able to speak?''

"He did manage a few words, yes.''

"And did those few words include telling you who did it?''

"No, I'm sorry to say they did not. Although I did ask, he expired before an answer could be given." The inspector frowned. "But," I added, "and this is important, he did repeat once again to being at the Bramwells on the night of the murder, although at the time he had no knowledge that a plot was afoot to kill the man. And, that the murderer of Edgar Bramwell was the same man who had plunged a knife into his chest.''

"He said all that?" questioned the inspector with a face that registered a measure of skepticism if not bemusement.

"Well," I hedged, "in words to that effect.''

"And Mrs. Warner," he asked, "she will substantiate what you have said?"

"Oh, yes, certainly."

The frown returned, followed by a despairing shake of his head. "I still find it hard to believe a connection exists between the two murders. To be honest with you, I'd be just as happy to write up a report stating the cause of Zambini's death was due to person or persons unknown and let it go at that."

"Would you really, Inspector?" I asked.

He looked at me for the longest moment. "No, Mrs. Hudson," he said at last, "probably not. But you know what this new information of yours means, don't you? A reopening of the case," he answered glumly. "Which, needless to say," he went on, "isn't going to sit too well with my superiors down at the Yard."

"Then you accept the fact that Arthur Moore was not the murderer of Edgar Bramwell?"

"Aye. I'll suppose I'll have to if I'm to believe Zambini," he answered with eyes fixed on fingers of flame within the grate. "And why should I not? What reason had the man to lie?" he asked, returning his attention back to me.

I took his question to be rhetorical and made no reply other than to ask whether he had made any official announcement to the press in regard to Arthur Moore being the guilty party, as he had originally believed.

"No," he stated, "I can be grateful for that at least. Thanks to you," he added with a knowing smile in recognition of my having previously asked him to hold off doing so.

Catching him in this more congenial mood, I was

quick to press my advantage. "Inspector," I said, "I have a favor to ask of you."

"Oh, aye, and what would that be then?"

"I should like you to see to it that all our suspects in the case be at the Bramwell residence by eight o'clock tonight. Unless," I added somewhat face-tiously, "you are of a mind to cart both Mrs. Warner and me off to Scotland Yard for the murder of Max Oliver."

"Oh," he chuckled, "I don't think there's any chance of that. My questions were merely routine procedure, Mrs. Hudson. Besides," he added, "whatever would Mr. Holmes say, eh? Now, as to this meeting tonight you speak of—its purpose be-ing—?"

"To give a demonstration," I informed him, "as to how the murder at the Bramwell residence was committed."

"What! You're not saying you actually know how it was done?"

"I believe I do, Inspector," I stated most author-itively in a voice that belied whatever lingering doubts still remained.

"Right, then," he replied, edging forward on his seat, "what's your theory?"

I was completely taken aback by the question, though in hindsight I suppose I should have realized he'd ask it. "Ah, well, you see, Inspector," I fudged, "if I were to spell it out for you it might sound fanciful indeed." Which in itself was true. "But I believe that when you actually see how it's presented you'll be of a different mind."

The good inspector looked most displeased. "Oh, I see," he stated, "I'm to be kept in suspense as well, am I? Now, look here, Mrs. Hudson, these people would be under my authority. Should anything go awry it would be Scotland Yard who would look the fool. I'm sorry, I can't accept the responsibility of it.''

"Inspector MacDonald," I stated simply but firmly, "what we would have at best, is a number of people who have been inconvenienced for an evening. The alternative being, a conclusion to the case. It's as simple as that.''

He pondered the thought for a moment or two. Obviously I had struck the right chord, for he asked, "Would you want Miss Armstrong-Jones there as well? What with her recent bereavement—''

I breathed an inward sigh of relief. For by putting the question to me he had, in his own way, signaled his agreement to my proposal. "Yes," I replied, "I should like very much for her to be there. And the MacPhails," I asked, "you know where they're lodged, do you?''

He answered that he did, adding that since his unexpected meeting with them outside the shipping office they had been kept under constant surveillance, right up to the time of Arthur Moore's suicide. "I thought we had it pretty well wrapped up at that point," he said. "Even at that, it wouldn't surprise me to learn they're in league with this Burke chap. I haven't changed my mind on it being some sort of conspiracy between the lot of them. Strange," he added quietly on returning his gaze back to the fireplace.

"Strange? What is?" I asked.

"The games the mind can play on you.''

"How so?''

"The flames," he answered. "It's as if they had the power to put one into an hypnotic spell if you stare into them long enough."

"An hypnotic spell?" I repeated. "Keep that thought in mind for tonight, Inspector," said I, secreting a hidden smile. Not knowing quite what to make of my last remark, he smiled vaguely and let it pass, adding only that it was high time he was on his way.

After once more receiving his assurance he would meet with me at the Bramwells that very night, I walked him to the door, thanked him for his cooperation, and bade him a good afternoon.

Following his departure I returned to my kitchen, sat myself down, and proceeded to write out a step-by-step summarization of how I believed it was possible for our "invisible man" to carry out the murder of Edgar Bramwell in front of a roomful of people with apparently unseeing eyes. On rereading what I had written I was, up to a point, satisfied with the initial outline. I say up to a point, for I still had one or two conspicuous blank spaces that I hoped, and/or believed, would be filled in by Mr. Wooley.

On Vi's return the first thing I asked was "Is he coming?"

"Who? Mr. Wooley, you mean? Yes," she answered, "and quite excited about it he is, too. Said he'd meet us here at seven just like you asked."

"And Mr. Muir," I questioned, "you made it over to the Royal Geographical Society to speak to him as well, did you?"

"Aye," she answered, "but I had to wait in his outer office a good half hour 'fore his secretary, snooty thing that it was, would let me in to see

him.'' She then related in detail what he had to say
with regard to the questions I had asked her to put
forward. His answers proved what I had only recently begun to suspect. I afforded myself a small
smile of satisfaction in the knowledge that I was at
last moving in the right direction. ''By the way,'' I
informed her, ''I had myself a visitor today.''

''Who was that, then?''

''Inspector MacDonald,'' I answered. ''It seems,''
I continued, still somewhat bemused by it all, ''he
was looking for two very suspicious ladies who had
left the scene of a murder last night.''

''I knew it!'' she blurted out, startling me. ''I just
knew it, I did. Told you we should never have left
like we did. Now, what, I wonder?''

''Not to worry, Mrs. Warner,'' I hastened to assure her. ''The inspector, I'm happy to say, has decided to overlook our hasty departure. Not only
that,'' I added, ''but he's agreed to my proposal for
a meeting tonight at the Bramwell residence as
well.''

''Well, I'm glad to hear that, at least,'' she answered with a notable sigh of relief. ''Told him
about the broken glass from the goggles, did you?''
she asked as an afterthought.

''Actually, no,'' I replied. ''I thought it best to
keep one or two things to ourselves for the time
being.''

As for the remaining hours of the day they seemed
to fly by and by seven o'clock that night, both Vi
and I found ourselves waiting patiently in the parlor
for Mr. Wooley to put in an appearance.

''That'll be him now,'' remarked my companion,

rising to her feet as a brisk rat-tat-tat at the front door announced his arrival.

"Come in, come in, Mr. Wooley," I sang out as he made his way from entrance to parlor accompanied by Violet. "It was good of you to come. Sit yourself down."

"I did say you could call on me at any time, Mrs. Hudson," he answered with a smile. "Now then," he went on, settling himself into the chair occupied earlier that day by the inspector. "I understand from Mrs. Warner that you believe I can be of some help to you with this Bramwell case you're working on. Is that right?"

"True enough," I answered.

"Well, like I say, I'll be glad to help out in any way I can. But," he added, scratching his chin, "just how much help I can be, I don't know. I'm no detective, you know."

"I quite understand," I answered. "However, this doesn't involve whatever sleuthing abilities you may or may not possess. What I'm interested in is your expertise in one particular area."

"I got'cha," he replied with a knowing nod. "Still have a question or two about hypnosis, right?"

"I do indeed. But, here, let me explain," I went on, leaning forward to pick up my writings from the table. "What I've done is to set down on paper my theory as to how I believe the murder was committed."

"Mrs. Hudson, here, is a great one for writing out little notes to herself," my companion dutifully informed the man. "Ain't that right, Em?"

"Yes, well, be that as it may," I carried on,

"there are one or two questionable areas in which I
thought you—''

"Whoa! Back up there for just a minute," interjected Mr. Wooley. "You're saying you know how
it was done?"

"Yes, I believe I do," I answered.

"Well, I swan!" he exclaimed. "Go on, then,"
he urged. "Let's hear it."

I then proceeded, with but an occasional glance at
my notes, to give an oral account of what I believed
had transpired, pausing at various times to question
Mr. Wooley whether such-and-such was possible or
whether this or that could be done. When I had finished the answers I had received were all I could
have hoped for and more. However, my sense of
elation was tempered by the thought that what appeared plausible on paper might be quite a different
matter when played out in the Bramwell drawing
room.

"All I can say," he announced when I had concluded, "is if that's how it was done it was a mighty
slick piece of work."

"Aye, well, that's how we figure it. Right, Em?''

How *we* figure it, did she say? Nevertheless, for
the sake of harmony I smiled sweetly and nodded in
silent agreement.

"There was one thing though, I was wondering
about, Mrs. Hudson," continued Mr. Wooley.
"When you talked about 'the murderer did this and
the murderer did that' is there someone in particular
you have in mind?"

"Actually," I admitted, "there is a certain party
who I suspect. And while I do have evidence, both
concrete and circumstantial, I would need some sort

of overwhelming proof before I could definitely lay the charges where they belong. But, barring our luck in something turning up at the last minute," I added, "I'm afraid we'll just have to go along with what we've got and hope for the best."

"Well, what you've come up with so far sounds good to me," he replied. "As for Zambini, even though he's got himself mixed up in all this, he sure played his part like the old pro he is."

"Oh, you don't know, do you? But of course, how could you?" I replied on hearing him speak of the deceased in the present tense.

"Know? Know what?"

In answer to his question, Vi stepped in to give an overly lurid account of our discovery of the late Great Zambini, as we had found him in his hotel room and the manner in which he had met his fate. Needless to say, Mr. Wooley's reaction was one of complete shock. Though not so much I hoped that it would dissuade him from accepting a certain favor that I now put forward. "Mr. Wooley," I said, "as Mrs. Warner may have previously informed you, we are to be at the Bramwells within the hour, where I'll be demonstrating how the murder was committed to the inspector as well as to those suspected of the crime. However," I added, "I cannot do it alone. I shall need the assistance of a professional such as yourself."

His reaction was one of puzzlement. "I'm not sure I understand," he said. "You want me to go along with you ladies tonight and perform some sort of hypnotic act? Is that what you're saying?"

"Not some sort of an hypnotic act, Mr. Wooley," I replied. "The same act as that performed by Zambini. Or, at least, as close an approximation of it as possible. I'm only sorry, for your sake as well as mine, it had to be on such short notice. However,'' I added, ''I can fill you in on the details on our way over there.''

''Oh, look at the time,'' sang out Vi with an eye toward the grandfather clock. ''We best get a move on.'' She rose to her feet and I followed suit. Mr. Wooley, for his part, remained seated.

''Looks like I'm going to have to disappoint you, Mrs. Hudson,'' he said, shifting uncomfortably about in his chair. ''I'd like to help out,'' he went on, ''but I was never more than a second-rate act and to perform after all this time in a swanky house in front of a lot of swells, I just don't think I—''

''Nonsense, my dear sir!'' I exclaimed with as much gusto as I could muster. ''You'll be splendid. Mrs. Warner and I have every confidence in the world in you.'' Although I may have laid it on a bit thick, I was frantic with the thought that if I couldn't persuade him otherwise, it was all over before I had even started.

''Do you really think I could do it?'' he asked, bringing himself up into a standing position.

''You put *me* under nice as you please,'' contributed Vi. ''Don't see as how it would be any different with that lot.''

''There, you see,'' said I.

''But, look here,'' he complained, ''these old clothes of mine—I can't go over there looking like this.''

''You've nothing else?'' I asked.

''Just my Mr. Happy clown suit,'' he replied.

''Oh, that would do it, that would,'' muttered Vi.

"Two old ladies and a clown showing up to solve a murder."

"You'll just have to go as is," I stated, hoping that would be the end of it.

He shook his head. "My first chance to go solo as a class act and I turn up looking like Harry the Hobo? No, I couldn't," he said.

"Mr. Holmes!" exclaimed Vi.

"Where?" asked Mr. Wooley.

"No, not where," she said. "I mean, his suit. Mr. Holmes's suit. Those old clothes you fixed up for the church," she continued, turning to me. "Still got 'em, have you?"

"Yes," I was quick to reply, being quite caught up in the idea. "They're in a bag beside the bed. Good thinking, Vi," I beamed.

"Mr. Holmes's suit?" questioned Mr. Wooley, not knowing quite what to make of it all.

"We've made up a bundle of old clothes to take over to the church," explained Violet. "Including one of Mr. Holmes's old suits. And very nice it is, too. You might's well have it as someone else."

"You mean I can keep it?" he asked in little-boy fashion.

"I don't see why not," I answered. "You're about his same height and weight. It should do just fine. Now then, you get yourself into the bedroom and change into them. And Mr. Wooley," I added with a nervous glance toward the grandfather clock, "do hurry."

Off he went, quite pleased with the whole idea only to poke his head round the bedroom door but a minute later. "Ah, about Mr. Holmes's cap, Mrs.

Hudson,'' he asked, somewhat hesitantly, ''you know, the one with the flaps—do you think I—?''

''Just the suit, Mr. Wooley,'' I answered with an amused smile. ''Just the suit.''

TWELVE

A Game of Murder

⟳ OUR LITTLE PARTY of three finally arrived at the Bramwells' at twenty minutes past eight and were promptly shown into the drawing room by Martin where, much to my chagrin, we found all assembled and waiting.

"Ah, there you are, Mrs. Hudson," Jane Bramwell said on coming forth to greet me. "And Mrs. Warner, too," she added in a smile of acknowledgement. "How nice to see you both. But I do wish, Mrs. Hudson," she remarked pleasantly enough even though I sensed an underlying measure of irritation, "you could have let me know about tonight. I was only just informed of this meeting but a few hours ago by the inspector."

"Do forgive me, Mrs. Bramwell," I responded most apologetically. "But the events of the last

211

twenty-four hours precluded any chance I had of contacting you.''

''I see,'' she answered with a thoughtful nod. ''Yes, of course. And this gentleman is—?'' she asked with an eye toward the third member of our trio, who stood looking a trifle nervous in his newly acquired pin-striped suit which, I'm happy to report, fit him quite nicely indeed.

''Mr. Wooley,'' I answered. ''An assistant, if you will. Mr. Wooley,'' I said by way of introduction, ''Mrs. Bramwell.''

''Pleased to meet you, ma'am,'' said he.

''Mr. Wooley,'' she responded with a slight but nonetheless polite smile before once more turning to me to ask if there was perhaps anything that I might require.

''Actually, there is, Mrs. Bramwell,'' I answered. ''I wonder if you could see to it that the household staff be present here as well.''

''You want—?'' Obviously my request had surprised her. ''Yes, well, if that's what you wish,'' she complied. ''Oh, and Mrs. Birdie—?''

''Yes, if it's no trouble.''

''No trouble at all,'' she replied. ''I'll find Martin and have him see to it this very minute. If you'll excuse me then?''

''Don't think she liked the idea of you not telling her about tonight,'' confided Vi as the woman took her leave. ''Don't want to upset her, we don't, if you know what I mean. She's the one what's paying us.''

''When would I have had the time?'' I asked.

''So, that's my audience, is it?'' spoke Mr. Wooley, displaying little or no interest in our conversation as he took in those chattering away among themselves within the room. "Well, I've played to smaller crowds," he duly informed us. "I remember one time in Topeka—"

Whatever it was he remembered about Topeka (wherever that is) we never did find out for at that moment Inspector MacDonald who, I noticed, had up to that time been engaged in conversation with David MacPhail, approached us. "Ah, ladies, you're here then, are you?" was his redundant opening. "Still want to go ahead with it, do you, Mrs. Hudson?"

"I do indeed, Inspector," I answered, displaying what I hoped was a confident smile.

"I only hope you know what you're doing," he replied with a sorry shake of his head.

"Oh, you don't have to worry about Mrs. Hudson," Mr. Wooley informed him. "She knows what she's up to, all right."

"We can only hope," replied the inspector, adding, "I don't believe we've met."

"The name's Wooley," came the reply. "Peter Wooley. I'm here to lend Mrs. Hudson a helping hand, you might say."

"Hmmm," said the inspector. "American, are you?"

"True blue, through and through," was the proud reply.

"Hmmm," repeated the inspector.

It was no more than a few minutes later, I should think, when Jane Bramwell reentered the room with Martin, Mrs. Smollett the cook, Rose Tuttle the maid, and Mrs. Birdie the governess all trailing behind. As Mrs. Bramwell left the group to rejoin the others, her staff remained with their backs to the walls just inside the door, save for Mrs. Birdie who, on spotting me, came gushing forward. "Oh, Mrs. Hudson," she beamed, "it's ever so nice to see you again."

"It's good to see you again, Mrs. Birdie," I replied, returning the smile. "And how's our little girl?" I quipped.

"Dorothy? Couldn't be better. I've only now got her off to sleep but, as I was saying to her mother on our way in, if either one of us has to read her the story of Rumpelstiltskin one more time—" She rolled her eyes heavenward in mock anguish. "But, here now," she asked, taking in those assembled within the room, "what's all this about, eh?"

"I'll be explaining it all shortly," I informed her.

"I think you best get on with it now. Don't you, Mrs. Hudson?" queried a very impatient Inspector MacDonald.

Before answering, I took a quick scan around the room and saw that Vi, for her part, had moved off and was conversing with the MacPhails, while Roger Burke and Jane Bramwell were together in a corner hovering over a seated and decidedly pale Prudence Armstrong-Jones. No doubt the two were offering up their condolences on the death of her intended, Arthur Moore—as well I would have if time had permitted. However, I agreed with the man from Scotland Yard that we'd best get on with it. But, I might add, not before drawing him aside to inform him of the piece of broken glass I had found in Zambini's hotel room and the fact that it fit the lens of the driver's goggles that we had subsequently found in the Bramwell auto. Needless to say, the good in-

spector was not all that pleased on my having with-
held information from him.

"You have the broken glass?" he questioned me
in a growl.

"Yes," I replied with a tap to my purse, "in
here."

"And the goggles," he asked in much the same
manner, "where are they now?"

"In the motor car where we found them," I answered.

"Mrs. Hudson," came the exasperated response,
"I do wish—"

"Yes?"

"Oh, never mind," he answered in a resigned
sigh. "We'll speak of it later. But from what you
tell me, I'd best have Sergeant Formby retrieve
them. Now, where the devil is he?" he asked himself, surveying the room.

"If you're speaking of the gentleman in the brown
suit," I spoke up, "I believe we passed him in the
foyer on our way in here." After my receiving his
thank you, which sounded more like a grunt than
anything else, he turned on his heels and made for
the door.

Seeing that Mrs. Bramwell and Mr. Burke had
taken their leave of Miss Armstrong-Jones and,
having a minute or two to spare until the inspector's
return, I left Mrs. Birdie and Mr. Wooley to their
own devices and made my way over to the lady
where I dutifully expressed my sympathies on her
bereavement. Within a minute or two of the inspector's return, I excused myself from her presence and,
on crossing back, set my shoe down on something
underfoot. I picked it up and discovered it was Jane

Bramwell's locket. It would appear she never did get Martin to see to its defective clasp. Because I clutched it a little too tightly, the lid accidentally flipped open, revealing a photo that had obviously been cut down to fit inside its oval interior. One look at that photograph left me with a sudden sense of overwhelming relief if not giddiness. I snapped the lid shut, deposited it into my purse, and made my way back over to the inspector. "Shall we begin?" I asked, scarcely able to control my euphoria. He looked at me a little oddly but nonetheless nodded in agreement that we should.

He began by picking up an empty whiskey glass and klinking it a few times with his ringed finger in an attempt to signal the proceedings were about to begin. "Ladies and gentlemen," he announced when the chatter had finally died down, "before I go any further, I should like to thank each of you for coming tonight."

"Did we have a choice?" queried a male voice in a stage whisper that I recognized as belonging to Roger Burke.

Ignoring the odd snigger it elicited, the inspector pressed on. "As you know, Mrs. Hudson and Mrs. Warner, working in close cooperation with Scotland Yard," (I winced at that, but if it added to our credibility so much the better) "have been in the employ of Mrs. Bramwell, lending whatever assistance they could in regard to the tragic and, I might say, mysterious circumstances surrounding the murder of her late husband. We therefore thought it best to bring you up to date, as it were, as to where we stand in our investigation at the present time. I now turn the floor over to Mrs. Hudson."

"Thank you, Inspector," I said on making my way to the center of the room. "Ladies and gentlemen," I stated, "in reference to what you may have read in the daily tabloids, I, for one, do not believe in invisible men—be they murderers, or not." My remark garnered a chuckle or two. "Nevertheless," I went on, "I'm reminded of the old saying, there are none so blind as those who will not see. Or," I added, "cannot see." This time their faces remained blank and questioning. Oh, dear, I thought, I'm losing them. "Yes, well, in any event," I carried on, "I hope before this evening is over to not only show you how the murder was committed but, more importantly, who it was that did it." *That* certainly got their attention. After the general hubbub of voices had faded to a murmur, I continued. "What I should like to do, ladies and gentlemen," I stated, "is to reconstruct the events that took place prior to the murder."

"You mean the game of charades we were engaged in?" questioned Patricia MacPhail.

"Yes, exactly. Now then, before we actually begin, could I perhaps have Mr. Burke and Mr. MacPhail arrange the chairs in a semicircle in the center of the room as they were on the night in question?" After the two gentlemen had obligingly done so, all took their seats to the front of me. With the staff and Mrs. Birdie standing at the back of the room and Violet, Mr. Wooley, and Inspector Mac-Donald off to my side, I put it to my semicircle of suspects that there was one other person present that night. "At what time he entered," I said, "I have no idea. But," I added, "let us say for the sake of argument that it was during your game of charades."

"I say, hold on there a minute, Mrs. Hudson,"

spoke Roger Burke. ''Are you trying to tell us some-one actually sneaked into—''

''Sneaked?'' I interjected. ''No, not in the least, Mr. Burke. The gentleman would have, no doubt, been properly introduced to one and all by the one who saw to it that he'd be there.''

''And who would that be?'' he asked in what I can only describe as a condescending smirk.

''The murderer,'' I answered.

''Oh, really, Mrs. Hudson,'' announced Prudence Armstrong-Jones in a show of annoyance, ''this is too much. I, for one, can assure you there was no one else present within the room.'' The others echoed her irritation with a murmur of mumbling amongst themselves and a general shuffling about in their chairs. Would they announce an end to it before I started? I looked to the inspector for assistance.

''If you would bear with Mrs. Hudson for a little while longer,'' he stated as convincingly as he could, ''I'm sure she'll explain everything to everyone's satisfaction.''

''Aye,'' added Vi, ''everyone's satisfaction that is, but the murderer's.''

''But just who is this mystery person you speak of?'' questioned David MacPhail.

''The gentleman's name? Zambini,'' I answered.

''Zambini?'' chortled Roger Burke. ''Sounds more like the name of an African river.''

''Or someone's stage name,'' spoke Patricia MacPhail.

''It was indeed a stage name, Mrs. MacPhail,'' I stated. ''For you see, the Great Zambini, as he was billed, was a highly respected and professional hyp-notist.''

"A hypnotist!" she exclaimed. "But I don't understand—why is he not here? I should think that if he's involved—"

"Did you say *was* a hypnotist?" queried Jane Bramwell.

"Max Oliver, otherwise known as the Great Zambini," interjected the inspector in an effort to help quell the questioning voices, "was found murdered in his hotel room by a person or persons unknown not more than twenty-four hours ago," he informed one and all.

"Did you say murdered?" responded a startled David MacPhail.

"Indeed I did, sir," replied the inspector. "The gentleman," he continued, "having suffered a stabbing to the chest, was found by the ladies Hudson and Warner, lying in a semiconscious state before eventually succumbing to his wound."

"But what did this Zambini person have to do with us?" wailed an anguished Prudence Armstrong-Jones. "Oh, dear God in heaven," she moaned, burying her face in her hands, "it's all so—so horrible. Three dead now, including poor Arthur."

"Inspector MacDonald," announced a grim-faced Jane Bramwell, "I believe this has gone on long enough. I think we've heard all we want to hear about fanciful theories and murdered hypnotists. Mrs. Hudson," she continued, turning on me, "if this is the best you can do—"

"If you don't mind, Mrs. Bramwell," spoke the inspector, displaying obvious annoyance, "I should like Mrs. Hudson to carry on."

She said no more and I continued. "You asked me, Miss Armstrong-Jones," I said, after the woman had regained her composure, "what Zambini had to do with all this. The answer, dear lady, is far more than he realized at the time. Unbeknownst to him, he was merely being used as a pawn in a game of murder. To explain more fully," I continued, "let me set the scene if I may. Zambini enters and is introduced to those within the room as a famous hypnotist who is there to perform his act as part of the night's entertainment. However, it would not be his usual performance but one previously arranged by the murderer. Yet arranged in such a way that the hypnotist would have no idea what our murderer's real intentions were. I daresay he was being well paid and would voice no objection to a change in his routine. Now, I'm sure," I added, noting their puzzled yet rapt attention, "that everyone here, save the one who committed the deed, would like to see an end to all this tonight."

"Well, I jolly well would," announced Roger Burke. "And I'm equally certain I speak for the rest as well."

"Then with that thought in mind," I continued, "I'm sure no one would object to a demonstration I've arranged with Mr. Wooley, here. This gentleman," I added, motioning him to come alongside, "is a renowned hypnotist in his own right, having performed throughout England and the continent, as well as in his own country of America."

"Should have had you as my agent, Mrs. Hudson," responded my American friend with a smile in stepping forward.

"Are you asking us to be hypnotized, Mrs. Hudson—is that it?" questioned Patricia MacPhail.

"Yes," I answered. "If everyone is agreeable."

"I suppose if we declined it would look somewhat suspicious, wouldn't it?" queried her husband who, after a word or two with his wife, reluctantly agreed to go along with it.

"And you, Mr. Burke," I asked, "are you agreeable?"

"Whatever makes you happy, dear lady," he answered with an unconcerned shrug of his broad shoulders.

For her part, Miss Armstrong-Jones gave her consent as well, albeit somewhat hesitantly.

"Will you be wanting me to take part in this as well, Mrs. Hudson?"

"What I would like, Mrs. Bramwell," I answered, "is for you to take your place beside them in the role of an observer, as it were. You don't mind, do you?"

"Not a bit," she replied. "If you ask me, this whole hypnotism business smacks of nothing but witches and broomsticks. I'd just as soon sit it out."

"Oh, I think it will be ever so much fun," admitted Patricia MacPhail. "I've never been hypnotized before—why do you smile, Mrs. Hudson?"

"Let's get on with it, shall we?" I replied, sidestepping her question. "Mr. Wooley," I said, "anytime you're ready." He stepped forward and I stepped back.

"Thank you, Mrs. Hudson," he acknowledged with a slight bow before addressing the four seated subjects before him. "To allay any fears you may have, ladies and gentlemen," he began, "I can assure you this isn't going to hurt a bit. All you will feel is a sense of utter relaxation. In fact," he went on, "it might interest you to know a hypnotist is that one rare creature in show business who actually seeks to put his audience to sleep.''

With his quip earning him a chuckle or two, he carried on in much the same fashion with a few more light asides until he had them settled down into a more congenial and less apprehensive mood. When he believed the time was right, he went into his routine of telling them how relaxed and peaceful they were feeling until at last their heads began to slowly drop, one by one, onto their chests. ''Your arms,'' he continued, ''are now as heavy as lead. So heavy you cannot lift them. Try,'' he urged, ''try to raise your arms.'' Roger Burke attempted and, failing to do so, appeared much annoyed with himself. The others, faring no better, exhibited embarrassment if not outright puzzlement.

As he began his second phase of taking them deeper into their trance, I could only stand there and hope to high heaven he'd remember to ask the questions I had previously outlined for him. I needn't have worried. Seeing him standing there, center stage, as it were, he appeared to be in complete control and right on top of the situation.

''What I want you to do now,'' he told them, ''is to relive in your mind's eye the night of the murder. You will see it as clearly as you would a photograph. The scene's unfolding before your very eyes even as I speak, isn't it?'' There followed a silent nodding of heads from closed eyes. ''Edgar Bramwell is still alive—you see him there, don't you?'' Again, another nodding of heads in agreement. ''And where is he, exactly?'' he asked. ''Can anyone tell me that?''

Patricia MacPhail mumbled something or other.

"Yes, Mrs. MacPhail," he questioned, "you said—?"

"Back—of—us." Her words were slurred.

"I see," replied Mr. Wooley. "Edgar Bramwell is standing to the back of where you are all sitting, is that right?"

"No," she answered after a momentary pause. "He's—he's brought a chair over. He's sitting to the back of us."

"Sitting? He's taking part in all this as well, is he? Is that what you're saying?"

"Mmmm," she answered.

"Was that a yes, Mrs. MacPhail?" he asked.

She replied that it was.

"We're all looking," announced Prudence Armstrong-Jones.

"Looking?" he queried. "Looking at what?"

"Zambini," answered Roger Burke.

"I see, that's fine. You are all watching the Great Zambini perform. Can you tell me what he's saying or doing—anyone?"

David MacPhail, his brow now furrowed in thought, edged forward in his chair. "He's—he's telling us—" he announced before just as suddenly lapsing back into silence.

"Yes, go on, Mr. MacPhail," he urged the man. "What is it he's telling you?"

At Mr. Wooley's repeated requests, he at last spoke of them being told by Zambini that they would awaken on hearing the sound of hands clapping together three times and, on awakening, they would have no recollection of his ever being there. They would resume their game of charades with no knowledge whatsoever of there being a lapse in time.

It was at that point I allowed myself a smug little smile of satisfaction. All was going perfectly.

"And you are certain, all of you," pressed Mr. Wooley, "that he said on your awakening that no one would remember his ever being there. Is that right?" His question produced a mumbled chorus of yeses. "Nothing else?" he asked. "He told you nothing else?" They allowed that it was all they could remember.

I felt my heart sink. "But, there has to be something else he told them," I said, springing to Mr. Wooley's side. "There *has* to be!"

"You could be right," he answered. "I get the feeling they're holding something back although they may not be actually conscious of it."

"What are saying, exactly?"

"It's just possible," he answered, "that they were given a further posthypnotic suggestion or command that could only be triggered by their hearing some sort of key word."

"Is there no way of finding out what that word would be?" I asked, trying to control my emotions. For to have come this far only to have it revealed as some sort of parlor trick meant nothing.

"I could try putting them deeper," he suggested. "Then reask the question and see what we come up with."

"Yes, please do, Mr. Wooley," I was quick to answer. "For if we fail in this, then our demonstration, indeed, the very case itself, will have come to naught."

"I'll do my best, Mrs. Hudson," he answered reassuringly before once more returning his attention to the four faces before him. "You are now going to go much deeper within yourselves,'' he intoned, drawing them evermore into what I can only describe as a somnambulistic state. ''And as you do,'' he informed them, ''you will respond freely to any and all questions that I ask of you.'' Satisfied at last that they were now in a receptive mood, he asked if Zambini had given them a key word to remember. ''A word,'' he went on, ''that would be followed by a certain reaction on your part on hearing it.'' As they nodded slowly in unison that they had indeed been given such a word, I breathed a thankful sigh of relief.

''And what was that word?'' he asked.

Silence. Mr. Wooley tried again. ''It's all right,'' he soothed. ''You can tell me. You have nothing to fear. Everything is fine. Tell me the word and you'll feel better than you have ever felt before.'' Again, silence from his subjects. Only this time their faces were strained and grimacing, as if they were mentally engaged in mortal combat with their conscience.

''It's no use,'' spoke a dejected Mr. Wooley. ''Zambini's got them locked in tight. Locked in tight,'' he repeated. ''And from the grave at that,'' he added with a touch of pride, if not awe, for his former fellow performer. ''I'm sorry, Mrs. Hudson,'' he said.

''Then we are indeed lost, Mr. Wooley.'' I glanced over at the inspector and from the look on his face I could sense he was about to call a halt to the proceedings. ''Are you sure there's nothing else you can do to pry it from them?'' I asked again out of sheer desperation.

''I don't see what,'' admitted the man. ''And there's no use trying to guess. There must be a million words in the English language. Even though,'' he added, ''it would have to be a word that wouldn't be normally used in everyday conversation.''

''Why do you say that?'' I asked. ''Oh, I see. Yes, of course. If someone within the room spoke the word inadvertently, it would set off their reaction. It would have to be spoken by the murderer at the exact moment it was planned that they should hear it.''

''That's the way I figure it,'' he replied.

A word, I thought to myself, that no one would use if they spoke nonstop for a week—two weeks—a year. And I had but seconds to come up with it. I couldn't help but heave a sigh at the hopelessness of it all. It reminded me of—of course! That's it! It had to be! I had to control myself from giggling like a schoolgirl as I gave a tug to Mr. Wooley's sleeve. On lowering his head level with mine, I whispered the word in his ear. Hearing it, he gave me the oddest look.

''You're joking,'' he said.

''Try it,'' I answered. ''What have we got lose?''

''Shall I ask them if that's the word, or—?''

''No,'' I replied. ''Just say it. Their reaction will tell us if I'm right.''

After a clearing of his throat, he stepped forward to announce very dramatically, ''RUMPELSTILT-SKIN.'' All four gave a start, opened their eyes, blinked, and gazed somewhat vacantly around the room as if reorienting themselves to their surroundings.

''Well, I'll be jiggered!'' exclaimed Mr. Wooley.

I burst into a broad smile.

A gasp was heard from Mrs. Birdie from back of the room.

Jane Bramwell, seated in the fifth chair next to David MacPhail, looked decidedly uncomfortable.

On seeing the eyes of the four participants now fully opened, I asked Mr. Wooley if they were still "under," so to speak. He assured me as much, adding they would continue to be so until they heard the aforementioned clapping of hands. "Should I ask what Zambini had them set up to do on hearing the word?" he asked.

"That won't be necessary," I answered airily if not a little too smugly. "Let's play it out, shall we? I should like to talk to them. Can they hear me?"

"They're vaguely aware of someone speaking," he answered. "But I don't think they're quite focused in to—wait a minute. Ladies and gentlemen," he said on addressing them, "Mrs. Hudson would like a word with you. She will speak to you and you will hear her as clearly as you hear me." He turned back to me with a grin. "The stage is all yours," he said.

It was now or never. If they didn't react in the manner I was expecting, I'd look the perfect fool. But enough of negative thoughts, I told myself, there was only one way to find out. I squared my shoulders, took a deep breath, and began. "Miss Armstrong-Jones," I said, randomly singling out the woman, "do you see Mr. Wooley, here?"

"Do I see him?" She seemed quite perplexed by the question. "Why, yes, of course I do."

"And you, Mr. Burke," I asked, "can you tell me if you can see Inspector MacDonald within the room?"

"See him?" he questioned. "Why shouldn't I see him. He's standing there beside Mrs. Warner."

"You're quite right, Mr. Burke," I replied. "Quite

right. Mrs. MacPhail,'' I continued, ''you see me standing before you, do you?''

''Why, yes, of course, Mrs. Hudson,'' she replied with a smile, being somewhat amused by the question.

''And Mr. MacPhail,'' I asked, ''you see me as well?''

''Clear as a bell,'' he replied.

''See here, Mrs. Hudson,'' spoke the inspector on stepping forward, ''I really don't see where all this is leading.''

''Bear with me, Inspector.''

''Haven't I been?''

''One or two questions,'' I assured him, ''should wrap up this little segment quite nicely.''

''Get on with it then,'' he grumbled. A most impatient man, the inspector.

''Aye, don't stop now, Em,'' sang out Vi. ''You're doing right fine, luv.''

I smiled, gave her a little wink, and resumed my questioning, but not before asking Mr. Wooley how much longer they would remain in their trancelike state.

''I suppose I could keep them under indefinitely,'' he answered, ''if it comes to that. But I'll feel a lot better when I snap them out of it. Like I say, playing with the mind can be a tricky business.''

''Right, then,'' I answered. ''I'll try to make it as quick as possible. ''Mr. MacPhail,'' I said, directing my attention to the gentleman seated next to the lady of the house who, up to that time, had remained conspicuously silent, ''I wonder if you would do me a favor? Could you point out Mrs. Bramwell to me?'' On my stating her name, Jane Bramwell gave a bit of a start and, on seeing she was about to speak,

I pressed my finger to my lips in a gesture for her to remain quiet. I then watched in utter fascination, as did we all, as David MacPhail, with eyes darting about the room, continued to seek her out. "You don't see her?" I asked. He seemed somewhat confused and answered by shaking his head that he did not.

By this time, those in back as well as Vi and the inspector had moved in closer—the better to be a part of this intriguing display of mind over matter. "Turn your head to the right, Mr. MacPhail," I said. "Perhaps she's sitting in the chair next to you." He did as asked and while I and the others saw a Jane Bramwell sitting there with drawn face and trembling lip, David MacPhail answered that he could see no one at all. "What is it you do see?" I questioned.

"A chair," he answered. "I see a chair."

"And no one is sitting in it?"

He squinted his eyes into the face of the woman seated no more than an arm's length away and again repeated he saw nothing more than an empty chair beside him.

"Amazing," I heard the inspector whisper to the back of me.

"Perhaps the others may be able to help me out," I continued. "Mrs. MacPhail, Miss Armstrong-Jones, and you, Mr. Burke, could any of you tell me if you see Mrs. Bramwell anywhere within the room?" After they had obliged me by craning their necks this way and that and, in the process, looking squarely in the direction of Mrs. Bramwell from time to time, all confessed their inability to see her.

"Each one of you," I said, addressing the four, "were told by Zambini that on hearing the word

Rumpelstiltskin, there would be certain people whom your eyes would not see. They would pass before you, indeed, stand before you, and yet you would be unaware of their presence—isn't that true?" They solemnly agreed that it was. "And that, Inspector," I said, turning to the man from Scotland Yard, "is how the murder of Edgar Bramwell was carried out. You may bring them out of it now, Mr. Wooley," I said, being, I might add, quite pleased with myself.

My American neighbor then began the process of releasing them from their trance by telling them not only how relaxed and refreshed they'd be on awakening, but that they would remember everything they saw on the night Edgar Bramwell was shot. Then, with Mr. Wooley's clapping of hands three times in quick succession they awoke feeling, they admitted, no worse for the wear from their experience.

After all four had collected their thoughts, Patricia MacPhail, as if she could scarce believe it herself, was the first to announce that she now remembered everything that had taken place on the night of the murder. "Oh, Jane, dear Jane," she said, more sorrowfully than accusatory, "how could you have?" The others, as images of that fatal night seeped back into their mind, were equally aghast. As for the lady herself, she arose angrily to her feet to ask, nay, order, that the inspector put an end to it all. "Am I to stand here in my own home," she demanded to know, "and have my friends accuse me from images derived from nothing more than a parlor trick?"

"She's right, you know," remarked the inspector in turning to me. "I'm afraid we'd need more than an eyewitness account, if I may call it that, from four people who were under the influence of hypnosis. It would never stand up in court, Mrs. Hudson.''

I quite agreed with him and, after his restoring some sort of order to the proceedings, I announced that with his permission I should like to offer up a more detailed account of what occurred on the night of the murder.

''I'd not be lying if I said I'd be grateful if you would,'' he answered. ''After what I've seen here tonight I'd be much obliged to hear what exactly did take place.''

''Oh, Em here—Mrs. Hudson, that is,'' added Vi, ''will tell you what happened right enough. You might say we figured it out together. Right, Em?'' After giving her ego a lift by agreeing with her that such was the case, I addressed the room.

''Let us go back once again to the night of the murder,'' I began. ''This time,'' I added with a wry smile in Mr. Wooley's direction, ''in memory only. There is a party in progress given not by Mr. Bramwell who, I subsequently learned was not the party type, but by his wife. She arranges the guest list and, along with her accomplice''—at the word accomplice Jane Bramwell drew a sharp intake of breath but said nothing—''they set about seeing to the 'entertainment' as well. On the night in question the maid and the cook have retired for the night. Dorothy Bramwell is asleep in her bedroom, as is Mrs. Birdie, who has fallen asleep in a chair beside the little girl's bed. Martin is in and out of the drawing room seeing to the needs of one and all whenever called upon. Zambini enters. Mrs. Bramwell calls a halt to the game of charades they are engaged in to introduce him to her husband and guests as the great hypnotist that he is. Her husband and their guests, who have perhaps indulged in one too many, agree to take part in his act. With the exception, I might add, of Jane Bramwell. Once he has them under, Zambini tells them what he has been instructed to say—that when they awake they will have no memory of his ever being there and, that on hearing the word Rumpelstiltskin, Mrs. Bramwell and her accomplice would seemingly vanish before their eyes and would not be seen until they once more heard the word spoken. Having done his part and no doubt believing it all to be some sort of practical joke the lady of the house is playing on her guests, the hypnotist departs. Jane Bramwell claps her hands three times, they awake and blithley carry on with their game of charades with no knowledge of Zambini having ever been there or of a time lapse having occurred. That is, more or less, the way it happened, up to that point, isn't it, Mrs. Bramwell?''

"There's not a word of truth in it!'' she retorted angrily. "Not a word!''

"Carry on, Mrs. Hudson,'' spoke the inspector quietly yet firmly.

"Thank you, Inspector. To pick up where I left off,'' I continued, "Edgar Bramwell stands before them carrying out his part in their game by trying to mime the answer to the name of a particular book. His wife sees this as the perfect opportunity. If she calls out Rumpelstiltskin, and Zambini's posthypnotic command has no effect on them, who would be the wiser? Simply a wrong answer on her part. Nothing more, nothing less. Ah, but should it result in triggering the desired effect. . . . She calls out the name Rumpelstiltskin and, like as not, tests their reaction. Perhaps by waving her arms in front of them—or some such thing. Of course, in hindsight, we now know that Zambini did not disappoint her. She was as vaporous as air to them.

"One moment, Mrs. Hudson," spoke the inspector. "Before you go any further, just who or what is this Rumpelstiltskin you speak of?"

"Oh, I'm sorry, Inspector," I apologized. "Rumpelstiltskin is the title name of a gnomelike creature in a children's fairy tale. The name flashed through my mind when I realized Mrs. Bramwell needed a word that she could be sure wouldn't be spoken during the course of the evening's conversation. And what better word than the name of her daughter's favorite nursery story—a fact Mrs. Birdie and I can well testify to."

"A fairy tale. Yes, that's all it is. Everything Mrs. Hudson has told you, Inspector, has been nothing *but* a fairy tale!" snapped a most agitated Jane Bramwell. "I'm sorry," she continued, "but I believe I've been more than patient. Now I must ask you—all of you, to please leave."

"I'm sorry, Mrs. Bramwell, but this is a police investigation we're conducting. I'm afraid you'll just have to be patient a little while longer," was the man from Scotland Yard's unruffled reply.

"Then I believe I should have my barrister present."

"That, of course, is up to you. But for what purpose?" he asked. "You've not been charged with anything. Now then, Mrs. Hudson," continued the inspector after the woman had flounced angrily back to her chair, "you were saying—?"

"With Zambini's posthypnotic command now in

effect," I began again, "Mrs. Bramwell hurries to the door, opens it, and calls out to her accomplice, who enters and walks directly over to the group innocently engaged in their game of charades. A pistol is produced and is fired directly into Edgar Bramwell's chest. As the murderer makes a hasty retreat out of the room, Jane Bramwell once more calls out the key word and, as she does, all resume a state of full consciousness and, in so doing, see the body of their host lying dead on the floor in front of them."

"Ingenious," murmured the inspector. "With but one flaw, actually. Why would they not have seen this accomplice you speak of?"

"If you recall, Inspector," I answered, "Mr. Wooley's four hypnotized subjects informed me while under his, spell, shall we say, that they'd been given the names of certain people who would remain unseen to them."

"With these certain people, as you put it, being Mrs. Bramwell and her coconspirator. Is that what you're saying?"

"Yes, exactly," I replied.

"And this other person would be—?"

"Mr. Burke," announced Vi, quite unexpectedly. "Mr. Roger Burke, that's who. He never was hypnotized. Just pretending, like," she informed one and all. "It was him and her all along."

All eyes turned in Mr. Burke's direction as he sat there with mouth agape, looking both baffled and bewildered by the accusation. "Me!" he finally blurted out on finding his voice. "You think it was me! That's utterly ridiculous. I had no motive for wanting the man dead. Besides," he added, going on the defensive, "I saw what actually happened. I remember it all thanks to your Mr. Wooley. As do the MacPhails and Prudence.''

"Yes, Mr. Burke," I agreed, "you did indeed see what took place as did the others who will attest to your innocence. No, Vi," I added, on turning to my companion while silently wishing she hadn't taken it upon herself to suddenly blurt out his name, "it wasn't Roger Burke. You've forgotten, it seems," I went on, trying to soften the blow of her embarrassment, "that during your meeting with Mr. Muir of the Royal Geographical Society, he mentioned to you that Edgar Bramwell had informed him he had every intention of backing Mr. Burke's expedition— and this, not more than twenty-four hours before he was shot. It was Jane Bramwell who stated otherwise. Edgar Bramwell was the last person in the world that Mr. Burke wanted to see dead. And it was Jane Bramwell who fueled the fires with derogatory rumors with respect to Arthur Moore's reputation which ultimately led the man to suicide. Were the MacPhails involved?'' I asked rhetorically. "Hardly," I answered, 'lest Vi took the question as an opportunity to state otherwise. "The planning of such a complicated murder and all that it entailed would have had to be thought out over a period of time and the MacPhails as well as Mr. Burke had only arrived in England no more than a week or so ago. In any event, they could not have arranged a party at the Bramwell's, only Jane Bramwell could have done that. Besides," I added, "It was Patricia MacPhail's singular remark about believing she had heard some sort of noise that I believed indeed could have been a shot, that led Mrs. Warner to question whether they could have been drugged and I, from that, that the answer could lie in their having been hypnotized. Evidently, Patricia MacPhail had been a more difficult subject for Zambini to put completely under, as I believe is often the case. Regardless of that, it was hardly a remark a guilty person would have offered up. And was it not queer," I continued, "that Jane Bramwell, on seeing her husband had been shot, would not rush to her daughter's room to check in on the child? But of course there was no need, was there, Mrs. Bramwell? You knew your daughter was perfectly safe."

I now turned my attention to Mr. Burke. "It's quite true, sir, as you say, that you and the Mac-Phails and Miss Armstrong-Jones now remember all that took place on the night of the murder including who it was that acted in conjunction with Mrs. Bramwell. Perhaps you and the others would now like to point out that person to Inspector MacDonald."

"What!" cried out the inspector who appeared much taken aback by my remark. "You don't mean to say that person is here in this room?"

I said nothing, but watched, as did we all, as they turned in their chairs to face the back of the room and, in so doing, arms were raised in unison to point accusatory fingers at Peter Martin.

"They're saying it was this Martin chap—Bramwell's manservant?" The man from Scotland Yard appeared more than a trifle bewildered.

"Exactly, Inspector," I replied. "For who else could it have been? You see—"

"She's mad!" bellowed out the accused man from the back of the room. "Completely insane! It's as Mrs. Bramwell says, the whole thing is a fairy tale.''

"Aye, well, in your case," sang out Vi, who evidently felt she was now on firmer ground with her accusation, "it's a fairy tale without a happy ending for you, my man."

"My position doesn't call for me to stand here and listen to this," he retorted and, on flinging the door behind him open to make his exit, found himself confronted by Sergeant Formby holding, of all things, a brown paper bag in his hands.

"That gentleman has decided he's not leaving after all," announced the inspector in manner calm and collected. "Show him back in, would you, Sergeant? There's a good chap." The man did as he was told, stepping into the room himself as he did so and closing the door behind him.

"Aside from our 'so-called' eyewitnesses, you're sure about all this, are you, Mrs. Hudson?" queried the inspector.

In lieu of an answer, I posed a question. "When you arrived tonight, Inspector," I asked, "who saw you in?"

"Why, this Martin chap did," he answered.

"As did he when we arrived. And as he would have when Zambini arrived on the fatal night. Wouldn't you agree?"

"Yes, I daresay you're right."

"Martin, as he himself has stated," I went on, "was in and out of the room on several occasions that night. Yet, did he ever once mention to anyone that Zambini had been there as well? No. Why? The answer is obvious. The scheme of how to do away with Edgar Bramwell was entirely his idea. No doubt he had caught Zambini's performance at the theater. A performance that led him to the idea of how to do away with the man by combining hypnosis with murder.''

"Evidence, Mrs. Hudson," murmured the inspector. "Evidence."

Aside from Peter Martin not revealing the presence of the hypnotist, the only other evidence I had was the account offered up by the four Mr. Wooley had hypnotized. And, oh, couldn't the defense in any court of law make quick work of that. I had to get myself on firmer ground. "For the present, Inspector," I said, "let us move onto the murder of Max Oliver. Zambini's real name," I informed the uninformed who, on gathering round, stood as attentive as any audience on opening night. "In regard to that man's tragic demise," I continued, "I believe you mentioned the murder weapon as being a knife. Didn't you, Inspector?''

"Aye. A carving knife, as well you know, Mrs. Hudson," he smiled.

"True. And who," I asked, "would have access to such a knife?" I let the question hang there by turning to MacPhail and Burke to ask where they were currently lodged. "My wife and I have a room at the Dorset Arms," Mr. MacPhail informed me while Mr. Burke stated he was staying at the Hartford. "Hotels, Inspector," I announced, "where a carving knife would less likely be available to either gentleman than would, say, a private home such as this." The implication that Martin had purloined the knife from the Bramwell residence was not lost on the man from Scotland Yard. Nevertheless, I pressed on by asking Mrs. Smollett, the cook, who stood half-hidden behind Mrs. Birdie, whether she was aware of any missing cutlery.

"Why, yes I am," she declared. "A carving knife. I was looking for it only yesterday. Gave Rose, here, a great tongue-lashing, I did. Thought she had misplaced it. She's quite the one for losing things, is our Rose. Why, it was only last week—"

"Yes, thank you ever so much, Mrs. Smollett," I cut in. "You'll be happy to know that your carving knife is currently in the possession of Scotland Yard."

"And now you accuse Martin of this Zambini person's murder simply because Cook's lost her carving knife, is that it?" spoke Jane Bramwell. And while her face exhibited a contemptuous smirk the apparent uneasiness she was experiencing expressed itself in the continual clenching and unclenching of her hands.

"There's a little more to it than that, Mrs. Bramwell," I answered. "There was only one other person beside yourself and Martin who knew what had actually taken place that night. Zambini. And only then, by reading about it in the daily tabloids, did he fully realize the part he had played in it all. It is my belief, Inspector," I continued, "that both Mrs. Bramwell and Martin had badly miscalculated, if they had thought about it all, the extent of press coverage that would follow in the wake of such a bizarre murder. Did Zambini contemplate going to the police with his story in the hope of vindicating his part in it or was his plan to be one of extortion? Perhaps we shall never know. But as long as he remained alive they could never be sure of being found out. Zambini had to be taken care of permanently."

Peter Martin sprang forward. "It's all some sort of conspiracy. That's what it is!" he cried out. "They're all in this together. Mrs. Bramwell and I had nothing to do with any of it. You've got to believe me, Inspector."

"It makes no never mind whether I do or not," came the reply. "This isn't a court of law. But I will ask you to refrain yourself from any further outbursts. You'll have plenty of time to tell your side of the story when the time comes," added the inspector before indicating to me with a nod of his head that I continue.

I did so by stating that Martin had driven over to see Zambini in his hotel room with a knife at his side and murder in his heart. Once there, an altercation between the two followed, with the end result being the stabbing and ultimate death of Max Oliver, alias the Great Zambini. After the deed was done a hasty retreat was made down the fire escape to the waiting car.

"A motor car being used as an escape from a murder," mused Violet. "Whatever next, I wonder?"

"Why me?" cried out Martin, tossing the question to the air. "Why couldn't MacPhail or Burke have murdered him and driven the car back?"

"I should be very much surprised," I answered, "if either man can even drive a motor car, having spent a good many years abroad both in the Far East and Africa."

"First time I ever saw one," admitted David MacPhail, "was when we arrived back here in London."

"Can you imagine," added Roger Burke with a

wry smile, "trying to drive my way through a rain forest in one of those contraptions? No, I've no use for them myself. Couldn't drive one to save my life."

Peter Martin's body literally sagged under the weight of his guilt—even more so when I informed him I had found the broken piece of glass from his goggles in the hypnotist's hotel room. "Actually," I added, withdrawing the broken shard from my purse, "I have it right here."

"Yes, what it is, Sergeant?" questioned the inspector in some annoyance at the man's attempt to gain his superior's attention by a gentle tugging to his sleeve. "Speak up, man."

"The goggles, sir," stated the sergeant on removing them from his paper bag, "I have them here." When the broken piece I had in my possession was aligned to that of the remaining glass within the housing, it fit perfectly. "I also found this as well," he added, bringing forth a handgun from the same paper bag. "It was hidden under the front seat of the motor car."

"Good work, Sergeant," beamed the inspector.

"I swear to you, Inspector, Mrs. Bramwell and I are innocent of any wrongdoing," stated Martin. "What earthly reason could we have?" he asked, turning to me. "Can you answer me that, Mrs. Hudson?"

It was a question that caught the inspector's interest. He eyed me intently, awaiting my reply.

"Being aware," I began, "that there was never any mention of any items having been stolen within the room or, for that matter, within the house itself on that fatal night, the murder had to have been one of passion. There is a passion for love and a passion for hate. You loved Jane Bramwell," I said, addressing the man, "and you hated her husband, as did she, for his mistreatment of her. It was only natural for her to turn to you, the only other man in the house, for comfort and affection. Which in time turned to love. Edgar Bramwell was a wife beater and a bully, Inspector," I said on addressing him as well as those within the room. "The household staff and Mrs. Birdie can attest to that. Now," I went on, "one might say divorce would have been the more logical alternative to murder. But bear in mind, there are but a small percentage of women in England who ever file for such action on their behalf. And of those that do, few are granted. Of those that are, the wife rarely receives custody of the children. I am a woman of my times and I cannot say whether such laws are right or wrong. But with the female of the species having been known to add a spoonfull of arsenic to a teacup or two when finding themselves locked into a situation similar to Mrs. Bramwell's, it does lead one to specualte how many husbands might be alive today if the bill of divorcement was more favorably balanced between the sexes."

Jane Bramwell, harboring a sliver of a smile, spoke up. "Mrs. Hudson," she said, "while I couldn't agree with you more in respect to English laws regarding divorce, to say that Peter Martin and I are, involved, shall we say, is absolutely ridiculous."

"Is it?" I asked. "I'm an old woman, Mrs. Bramwell," I went on, "and not up to the current trends in today's society. But is it now fashionable," I asked, removing her locket from my purse, "for the lady of the house to keep a photograph of her husband's manservant round her neck?'' She gasped on seeing it and clutched at her throat. ''You should have had Martin see to its defective clasp,'' I added before handing it over to the inspector.

Her paramour immediately sprang to her defense. ''I put it there,'' he blurted out. ''Yes, that's it. She didn't even know that I—''

''Oh, Peter, for God's sake,'' wailed the woman, ''say no more. It's no use, no use,'' she moaned. ''They know too much.''

At that, Inspector MacDonald stepped forward to inform the pair that they would now be required to accompany him to the Yard where a formal charge of murder and conspiracy to murder would now be laid against them in regard to the deaths of Edgar Bramwell and Maxwell Oliver. A glum and dejected-looking Peter Martin was taken in tow by Sergeant Formby and led out of the room.

''My daughter, Inspector,'' pleaded the woman, ''I wouldn't want her to wake up tomorrow and find me not there. Could I but stay the night here?''

''I'm afraid not, Mrs. Bramwell.''

''Inspector,'' I asked on stepping in, ''what harm would there be in it? Surely, one night—?'' My concern was for the child rather than the mother.

He exhaled a deep sigh. ''Oh, very well, Mrs. Hudson,'' he said at last, and then, reluctantly, ''for your sake then. But mind you now, Mrs. Bramwell,'' he stated most officiously, ''I shall expect to see you in my office tomorrow morning at nine sharp.''

''Bless you, Inspector, and you too, Mrs. Hudson,'' was the woman's heartfelt reply before rushing out the door and up the stairs to the child's bedroom.

"Congratulations on a fine bit of detecting, Mrs. Hudson. You and Mrs. Warner and you, Mr. Wooley, can well be proud of yourselves," announced the man from Scotland Yard on Mrs. Bramwell's departure. "But bear in mind," he added before taking his leave of us, "I shall expect to see the lot of you in my office tomorrow as well."

"Oh, Mrs. Hudson, isn't it just awful," sobbed Mrs. Birdie on coming forward. Her eyes were red-rimmed. "Mrs. Bramwell to be taken away and her poor daughter—"

"What will happen to the child now?" I asked.

"I believe Mrs. Bramwell has a sister living in Kent," she replied. "I suppose Dorothy will be sent along there. It's all so sad, really."

"You knew, didn't you," I asked, putting the question more in the form of a statement.

"Knew—? You mean about Mrs. Bramwell and Martin being 'that way' about each other? Yes, well, that is to say," she hedged, "I had my suspicions. There's not much that goes on around here that I don't know about one way or the other. I won't be arrested, will I?"

"No, Mrs. Birdie," I answered with a smile. "You won't be arrested."

"They really were invisble, weren't they?" spoke Mr. Wooley after Mrs. Birdie had drifted off and out of the room.

"How's that again?" I asked.

"Jane Bramwell and Martin, they really were invisible," he repeated. "Just like the papers said—you know, about invisible murderers and all."

"I suppose in a way you're right," I answered. "At least they were to those within the room."

"One thing puzzles me, though."

"Oh, and what would that be, Mr. Wooley?"

"Why Mrs. Bramwell would hire you to find out who murdered her husband when she was part and parcel of it herself."

"Hardly the thing one would expect a guilty person to do, is it?" I answered.

"No, it isn't," he stated.

"Exactly," I replied.

"Oh," he said, pondering the thought.

"We can't win for losing, we can't," announced Vi, who evidently was harboring thoughts of her own.

"What's that supposed to mean?" I asked.

"Mrs. Bramwell," she said. "Think she's upstairs now writing out a check for our fee? Not ruddy likely she'd pay for the privilege of being charged in a murder. We've outfoxed ourselves. That's what we did."

"Yes, I suppose you're right," I admitted with a chuckle at the irony of it all.

"Aye, well, we're finished and done with it now and that's the main thing."

"Finished?" I repeated while noting Mrs. Smollett heading for the door. "Not quite," I added. "Mrs. Smollett," I called out. "One moment, if you please. Come along, Vi," I added on whisking her over to the woman.

" 'Ere, what's all this about, eh?" questioned my companion on our approach.

"Mrs. Smollett," I said, ignoring for the moment Vi's question as I addressed the woman, "I take it you've been a cook for a good number of years now. Is that right?''

''More than I care to remember, Mrs. Hudson,'' she answered with eyes that darted suspiciously between Vi and myself. No doubt the good woman was wondering if I was about to implicate her in the murder as well.

''There's a certain dish I make from time to time,'' I said, noting the relief in her face on realizing the nature of my inquiry. ''Toad-in-the-hole. You're familiar with it, are you?''

''Why, I should say I am,'' she replied. ''I've made it many a time. Why do you ask?''

''And if you were making it for no more than four,'' I asked with an eye toward Vi, ''how many eggs would be required?''

''Eggs? For four? Why,'' she said, ''it'd need no more than one.''

''*Now*, Mrs. Warner,'' I stated, trying not in the least to hide a smug little smile, ''*now*, it's over.''

ANN GRANGER

The Meredith and Markby Mysteries

"The author has a good feel for understated humor, a nice ear for dialogue, and a quietly introspective heroine."

London Times Saturday Review

COLD IN THE EARTH	72213-5/$5.50 US
A FINE PLACE FOR DEATH	72573-8/$5.50 US
MURDER AMONG US	72476-6/$5.50 US
SAY IT WITH POISON	71823-5/$5.50 US
A SEASON FOR MURDER	71997-5/$5.50US
WHERE OLD BONES LIE	72477-4/$4.99 US
FLOWERS FOR HIS FUNERAL	72887-7/$5.50 US
CANDLE FOR A CORPSE	73012-X/$5.50 US

DEN OF ANTIQUITY MYSTERIES

by
TAMAR MYERS

LARCENY AND OLD LACE
78239-1/$5.50 US/$7.50 Can

As owner of the Den of Antiquity, Abigail Timberlake
is accustomed to navigating the cutthroat world of rival
dealers at flea markets and auctions. But she never thought
she'd be putting her expertise in mayhem and detection to
other use—until her aunt was found murdered . . .

GILT BY ASSOCIATION
78237-5/$5.50 US/$7.50 Can

A superb gilt-edged, 18th-century French armoire Abigail
purchased for a song at estate auction has just arrived
along with something she didn't pay for: a dead body.

THE MING AND I
79255-9/$5.50 US/$7.50 Can

Digging up old family dirt can uncover long buried
secrets . . . and a new reason for murder.

IRIS HOUSE B & B MYSTERIES
by
JEAN HAGER

Featuring Proprietress and part-time sleuth, Tess Darcy

THE LAST NOEL
78637-0/$5.50 US/$7.50 Can

When an out-of-town drama professor who was hired to direct the anual church Christmas pageant turns up dead, it's up to Tess to figure out who would be willing to commit a deadly sin on sacred grounds.

DEATH ON THE DRUNKARD'S PATH
77211-6/$5.50 US/$7.50 Can

DEAD AND BURIED
77210-8/$5.50 US/$7.50 Can

A BLOOMING MURDER
77209-4/$5.50 US/$7.50 Can

Faith Fairchild Mysteries by Agatha Award-Winning Author
Katherine Hall Page

THE BODY IN THE CAST
72338-7/$5.99 US/$7.99 Can

THE BODY IN THE VESTIBULE
72097-5/ $5.99 US/ $7.99 Can

THE BODY IN THE BOUILLON
71896-0/ $5.99 US/ $7.99 Can

THE BODY IN THE KELP
71329-2/ $5.99 US/ $7.99 Can

THE BODY IN THE BELFRY
71328-4/ $5.99 US/ $7.99 Can

THE BODY IN THE BASEMENT
72339-5/ $4.99 US/ $6.99 Can